Bett...
Ir...

D0849680

[

Oh, My Goodness!

(more surprises from FairAcres)

Effie Leland Wilder

with illustrations by
Marilynn Mallory-Brandenburger

Ω

PEACHTREE

ATLANTA

Published by
PEACHTREE PUBLISHERS, LTD.
1700 Chattahoochee Avenue
Atlanta, Georgia 30318-2112

www.peachtree-online.com

Text © 2001 by Effie Leland Wilder
Jacket and interior illustrations © 2001 by Marilynn Mallory-Brandenburger

Jacket and book design by Loraine M. Balcsik
Book composition by Melanie M. McMahon

Manufactured in the United States of America

10 9 8 7 6 5 4 3 2 1

Library of Congress Cataloging-in-Publication Data

Wilder, Effie Leland.
   Oh, my goodness! : more surprises from Fairacres / by Effie Leland Wilder ;
with illustrations by Marilynn Mallory-Brandenburger.-- 1st ed.
      p. cm.
   ISBN 1-56145-255-6
      PS3573.I4228 O43 2001
      813'.54--dc21   2001003312

Dedication

I dedicate this book, with great pleasure, to the world's nicest publishing house: Peachtree Publishers, Ltd., of Atlanta, Georgia, and to all the lovely people who work in its halls.

They picked my original offering out of the pile of unsolicited manuscripts and pluckily decided to put it in print, even though I was a completely unknown author. I'm sure they felt they might be left with 4,900 copies of the first printing of 5,000 books—after my relatives and friends each bought a copy.

Well, it didn't turn out that way. The amazing sale of that little book and its successors has pleased them, and has been a wonderful boon to me, here at the tip-end of my life.

Ya-a-ay, Peachtree! Long may you publish.

—E. L. W.

Other books by Effie Leland Wilder

OUT TO PASTURE (BUT NOT OVER THE HILL)
OVER WHAT HILL? (NOTES FROM THE PASTURE)
OLDER BUT WILDER (MORE NOTES FROM THE PASTURE)
ONE MORE TIME (…JUST FOR THE FUN OF IT)

Author's Note

Soon after starting to write this book, my bad eyesight turned much worse. I couldn't see to type, and couldn't see my handwriting. I sent word to the publisher that I couldn't go on.

I had a call from Marian Gordin, my longtime editor. She begged me not to give up. She said, "Send me your scribbles. I will gladly decipher them."

So I sent her pages of scrawls. It was probably the first handwritten manuscript submitted to a publisher since Charlotte Brontë! Marian translated my squiggly words, and typed them neatly. She went beyond the call of duty. I will forever be grateful for her kindness, and for her patience with The Poor Old Soul.

I am also deeply indebted to my family and fellow "inmate" Betty Lee. Junior to me by several years, and with better eyes and ears, she has made herself invaluable by "reading back," by "looking up," and by being ready and willing to perform any service that a handicapped author might need. What a friend! *Merci beaucoup*, dear Betty.

Kudos are due to Vicky Holifield, the editor at Peachtree who was assigned to be my hand-holder and pusher and "let's-get-it-done" editor. She had a hard job, and did it with grace. I have not met her in person, but her voice on the telephone is mellifluous and was soothing to this aged, harried, one-foot-in-the-grave author.

—E. L. W.

Contents

<u>1</u>

Here We Go Again

August 5th

I went to the library at The Home this afternoon to see what new large-print books had come in. My eyesight has deteriorated so much that I even have trouble with large print, but I keep hoping someone will be able to design type I can read.

I promise, Dear Diary, that—this time at least—I did not go with the express intention of eavesdropping on my favorite joke-tellers, Paul and Curtis. But I had not been browsing at the table of new arrivals two minutes when I heard their familiar, hearty laughter. So I settled into my usual listening post, the comfortable armchair beside the window onto the terrace.

Paul was reading something aloud that someone had sent him on the Internet. It was about one of our favorite subjects here: old age. I pulled out my little notebook and jotted down as many of the funny lines as I could.

♣ You're getting old when you get the same sensation from a rocking chair that you once got from a roller coaster.

♣ Middle age is when you choose your cereal for the fiber, not the toy.

♣ Do you know why women over fifty don't have babies? They would put them down somewhere and forget where they left them.

♣ I finally got my head together, and my body fell apart.

♣ Time may be a great healer, but it's certainly a lousy beautician.

♣ Forget the health food. I need all the preservatives I can get!

Thank goodness we have humor to help get us through the daily ups and downs!

August 8th

Marcia Coleman and I decided to take a jaunt after supper (if two old critters hobbling on canes can be called "a jaunt"). My bad knees can't tolerate a lot of walking, but some exercise is required to keep them from getting stiff. A half-mile seems to be the comfortable amount.

We walked out of the front gate of FairAcres Home and turned right, toward "Kudzu Kottage," the house that Arthur Priest moved into five years ago. What a time that had been! Some of us had found this place (then covered in that "vine that ate the South") for Arthur and his wife, Dollie, to move into (and out of a tiny trailer) with their growing family. Their sons, Artie and Cliffie, were small, and baby Louisa was on the way.

All of us like to remember that time. It gave us a feeling of still being useful, especially dear Louly. Arthur was a beloved worker in the Maintenance Department here who couldn't drive a car—or any of The Home's vehicles—because he couldn't pass the driver's test. He couldn't read.

Many of us said, "What a pity!" But none of us did anything about it—except Louly Canfield. She had been a teacher. She got hold of some books on dyslexia—Arthur's trouble. At five o'clock after work every day, she worked with Arthur and taught him to read. He got his license, and eventually he became head of our Maintenance Department.

As Marcia and I approached the cottage, we saw Dollie sitting in the porch swing and Arthur sitting on the steps, with his back against the railing, surrounded by his children. He was reading aloud from a large book. The children looked up at him, absorbed. Every now and then they would all laugh.

We were just getting ready to turn around and head back toward FairAcres when Arthur's voice boomed out part of the story:

> "Aye, aye, mates," said Long John Silver, who
> was standing by with his crutch under his arm,
> and at once broke out with the words—
> "Fifteen men on the dead man's chest—"
> And then the whole crew bore chorus—
> "Yo—ho—ho, and a bottle of rum!"

The Priest children laughed and repeated gleefully:

> "Fifteen men on a dead man's chest!
> "Yo—ho—ho, and a bottle of rum!"

How wonderful to see, and hear, them enjoying *Treasure Island.* Marcia and I knew from our own pasts that those children would never forget their father reading to them on the front steps.

Blessings on you, Louly Canfield, I thought. *Your kind act will echo down the years.*

August 9th

Thinking about Louly always reminds me that there is much kindness in this place. The Golden Rule is alive and well. In fact, I honestly believe there is more thought of doing kindnesses "unto *others*" than of being "done unto."

A case in point. When Millicent de Parle was widowed and came here last year, she was pathetic—a lost, forlorn little creature. She had been spoiled, pampered, wrapped in cotton-wool, first by her mother and then by her husband. They'd never had any children, and she was alone when she moved here, and utterly helpless. She couldn't cope with getting herself dressed on time, with getting to meals, with adhering to any kind of schedule. Some of us tried to help her, but she remained forlorn and pathetic—until Eugenia took over.

Eugenia Prentiss is the widow of a Presbyterian minister. What a perfect "preacher's wife" she must have been: big-hearted, comfortable, and comforting.

Eugenia took Millie in hand, firmly. She took her to meals, and saw that she ate; she got her clothes all spruced up and took her to the beauty parlor for a badly needed hairdo.

As the months went by Eugenia arranged for Millie to join a Bible class and a knitting class. She invited people to her apartment for tea, to get to know Millie better. It was amazing and gratifying to see the shy creature blossom.

One morning, Eugenia knocked on Millie's door, and there was no answer. She opened the door and looked in.

There was a still form on the bed. It was Millie, and she was dead.

The doctor said she had apparently died very peacefully in her sleep.

Eugenia took up a collection and bought flowers for the funeral, and to put on the grave. She was quiet for days. She missed having sweet Millie to mother and advise.

About a month after the burial, Eugenia received a phone call from a gentleman who identified himself as Robert Remington, a Charleston lawyer. He said, "I am calling about the last will and testament of Mrs. Millicent de Parle. It contains a codicil written three months before she died. The codicil is dated, witnessed, and signed. Perfectly legal. It reads: 'To my dear friend Eugenia Prentiss, because of her kindness to me, I wish to leave my ruby ring and the sum of twenty-five thousand dollars.'"

Eugenia said she almost dropped the phone. "Twenty-five *thousand* dollars?"

"Yes, ma'am. Congratulations. I'm sure it is deserved. As soon as the legal process has been completed, I will come to see you and bring you the ring and a cashier's check for the money."

Eugenia was stunned. She kept saying, "That dear little lady. But I really didn't do anything."

We assured her that she had done plenty—that she

had made the last year of Millie's life not only bearable, but at times actually happy.

We knew that Eugenia had always longed to travel, and had never had the money. She had been the daughter of a minister as well as the wife of one. The churches in question had been small, and had paid low salaries. She had been obliged to scrimp, to "make do," to "eke out" all of her life, buying her clothes from thrift shops, and never traveling any distance on a vacation. Millicent had apparently recognized the situation and had made this wise and generous decision. Instead of leaving everything to relatives and established charities, she had opted to beautify and expand the horizon of someone whose selfless kindness thoroughly deserved it…to add a little frosting to what had been a plain, if useful, life.

Now Eugenia could start making joyous plans. She had always wanted to see Hawaii. Now she could go to those lovely islands—and could even afford to take someone with her.

She told me, "I've always thought it—now I know it: Cast your bread upon the waters, and it will come back *buttered!*"

August 12th

In walking down the halls at this home for retired people, if you're polite and ask people, "How are you?"

there's no telling what you'll hear. Some people just man-age a slight grunt. Some give you an "organ recital." After a while, you learn which people not to ask at all—unless you have all day to listen. If a new resident happens to ask after the health of one of these particular folks, you learn to make a quick exit, thinking, "Here we go again!"

One woman always responds to "How are you?" by say-ing, "I'm so as to be about." One man always says, "I'm tol'able." I suppose he means tolerable, meaning he can tol-erate his existence. My goodness! Just tolerate it? I want to celebrate it—just being alive! I want to hang on to life and squeeze every drop of experience and enjoyment out of it.

I'm no Pollyanna. I'm well aware of the griefs and aches and pains that come with aging. I creak with some of them myself (and I know I complain about my poor eyesight and knees to you, Dear Diary). But I'm trying to cultivate "an unconquerable soul" that can handle any-thing. Tol'able? No. I'm *fine, thank you.*

August 14th

Overheard (from a hearty eater at the table):

"Oh, no, not Jell-O again. Nothin' to it. You don't get anywhere. I'd just as soon try to eat moonlight!"

That reminded me of a comment my daughter, Nancy, once made. She said that raising teenagers was "like nailing Jell-O to a tree!" She was describing some disappointment with one of my dear grandchildren, who—I'm sure—were always on their best behavior when they came to visit me.

I often have to stifle a chuckle when observing my children raising their children. Brings back many fond memories of my sweet Sam, who was always very tolerant and patient—more patient than I was.

Luckily, I have a wonderful son-in-law, who has many of the same good qualities that my late husband had. I bless the day my daughter married him. He is not only good to her and the children, he is good to me!

He comes to see me, and he observes. Then he goes out and buys things to make me more comfortable: a darker-writing pen, a louder-ringing telephone, a clock with larger numbers.

As you know, Dear Diary, I call him my favorite son-in-law, which I can do with impunity, since he is my only one. He calls me his favorite mother-in-law, but he always adds two words: "so far."

I remember an old song: "A Good Man, Nowadays, Is Hard to Find." I tell Nancy to straighten up, fly right, and hold on to that good man.

August 17th

I have been bowled over by the reception given to my little books about life and laughter in a Southern retirement home. I've received more than 1,400 letters. They've come from every state and three foreign countries!

I've never written but one "fan" letter to an author. I wrote to Harper Lee, author of *To Kill a Mockingbird.* I remember getting a nice reply from her. That memory and a very real feeling of gratitude have prompted me to answer each missive. At first I sent personal notes, but now that my eyesight is so bad, friends usually have to read me the letters, and then I have to scrawl my signature to photocopied replies.

Some of the letters I receive are so lovely they make me cry. Some of them have given me good laughs, which I'm sure the writers intended.

One recent writer said, "You've inspired me to write the story of my life. I'm having a good time doing it. I didn't realize how interesting I am!"

Bless her heart.

August 20th

How good it is to be living among people of my own era! When you talk about Billy Sunday, or Chautauqua, or Amos and Andy, or Hadacol, you don't have to stop and explain.

Today we talked at breakfast about cold mornings a long time ago. (We could talk freely. No men had come to our table this morning.)

"I didn't wear a union suit," said Eloise, "but I remember wearing something called an 'underbody.'"

"I did, too," said someone else, "and below the underbody, you wore drawers—not panties. Sometimes the drawers were scratchy."

We talked about woolen caps, with ear flaps, and Buster Brown shoes.

"I had weak ankles," said Esther, "and my mother made me wear high-top shoes. I was mortified. Nobody else wore them, and they were hard to button. I had to use a buttonhook!"

We all nodded, remembering buttonhooks...remembering winter mornings, dressing in front of the "trash burner," dreading to go to the cold bathroom.

"Children just don't *know* these days," said Mabel. "Everything is warm and smooth for them..."

"I don't know about that," said Trudy, slowly. "When you think about traffic, and terrible crowds, and drive-by shootings, and guns in the classroom—I'm kind of glad I grew up when I did."

We grew thoughtful. Maybe we had grown up in a better world, but my children don't think so. They prefer this era of penicillin and heart bypasses, and television and fast jets. I wonder if they will have any soft memories of this fast-moving time.

When our conversation resumed, Esther talked about

the old blue-enameled coffee pot that sat on the back "eye" of her family's wood stove for so many years. "I can still smell it," she said.

"When Mama finally got a gas stove, the old wood stove was put out in the backyard. She kept asking Papa to cart it away.

"'I like to look at it,' Papa would say. 'Seems like I haven't had a decent biscuit since you got that fancy gas thing.'"

August 21st

In the Country Store today, the talk was about names. Hazel Watkins had just received the birth announcement of a new great-niece.

"They've gone and named her Sophronia," said Hazel. "Of course, that's what her mother and grandmother are named, but that doesn't make it right. That poor little girl...Sophronia!" She sighed as she put the announcement away in her bag.

"I think it's nice when a child is given a family name," said Christine Copeland, a delightful lady who has just moved here from Florida to be near her children. "There's history in it—and continuity—and meaning..."

"That's all right," spoke up Zeke Barron, "unless you had a great-grandfather with a name like Ezekiel Montgomery Barron."

"Which makes you Ezekiel Montgomery Barron the Fourth!" said Fred, taking a bite of his ice cream.

"Sounds aristocratic to me," said Hazel. "When I was a teenager I longed for a high-flown name—Honoria, or Celeste, or—"

Martha broke in. "Celeste reminds me of a story. My mother was interviewing a girl for a maid-of-all-work job. She asked her name.

"'My name is Celestial Star Simpson,' the girl said.

"'Oh, my!' said Mother. (She told me later that she couldn't see herself saying, 'Celestial Star, take out the garbage, please.') Then she had an idea. 'What do they call you at home, for short?' she asked.

"The girl went into a fit of giggles. 'They call me Sweetie,' she answered. Mother decided not to hire her."

"My mother said she played with a little girl named Truly I Love Thee Irene," said Hazel.

We whooped.

I asked, "Did they call her Irene?"

"No," said Hazel. "Mama said they called her Truly."

August 24th

Yesterday was a red-letter day. Julia Motte's handbag got emptied!

We had all wondered, for ages, about Julia's bag. She was never without it. Wherever she went—to meals, church, plays, walks on the campus—there it hung from her arm—a large affair made of strong cloth. It was jammed so full it looked as though it would burst at the seams. If it had been made of leather, she wouldn't have been able to get nearly as much in it. People wondered if she carried it to bed with her, and into the bathroom!

Julia and I are tablemates this session. Yesterday, as we were finishing our dessert, she wrapped up extra cookies in her napkin and picked up her bag from the floor beside her chair.

"Oh-oh," she said. "I guess I'll have to break down and empty this thing. I can't get these cookies in!"

She pushed her plate away and started pulling things out of the bag and onto the table.

We sat bug-eyed. Here came not only a coin purse and wallet, a notebook, pencils and pens—the usual inhabitants of handbags—but with them came a congregation: old theater programs, a deck of playing cards, rubber bands, paper clips, two nail files, pennies and dimes, a few dozen Kleenexes, and one of The Home's teaspoons.

This last seemed to bother Julia inordinately.

"Oh, my goodness! I didn't know I had this spoon!" She started polishing it with her napkin and looking embarrassed.

We were finding things much more interesting than the spoon. There was a cellophane "baggie" with three slices of bacon in it; there was a chicken leg wrapped in a paper napkin and getting a little "fragrant." There were packages of mints, chewing gum, and crackers. There were newspaper clippings and keys of many sizes.

"Well, would you look at this?" said Julia. "Here's the key to my cedar chest! I've been looking for it for six months at least."

People wandered over from other tables. There had been Home-wide speculation and wonder about Julia's handbag. One of the male residents said, "I'll bet she's got a handsaw in that thing!" Another one said, "Or a harmonica." Still another speculated as to whether she might have a flask of something.

Julia just smiled at everyone and didn't seem to mind the gawking.

"Thank goodness," Retta whispered to me, pointing to the chicken leg. "Now we won't have to call in the Health Department!"

Julia turned her "carpet bag" upside down, gave it a shake, and said, "I won't put everything back in. My arm was getting kind of tired."

2

Wit and Wisdom

August 27th

Curtis and Paul had a session on the terrace today, and I was at my window listening.

"I remember a story that Dizzy Dean used to tell," said Curtis.

"Tell it," Paul said. "I always got a kick out of Dizzy, both as a baseball player and later when he used to help broadcast games on TV."

"Well," Curtis recounted, "after he became famous, Ole Diz was driving through Arkansas one hot day in his large car, which was equipped with that brand new gadget: an air conditioner. A local fellow thumbed a ride with him, saying he was only going into town a few miles down the road.

"After about two minutes, the man turned to Dizzy and said, 'Hey, friend, how 'bout lettin' me out? It's done turned off so cool I think I'll go home and kill some hogs!'"

We all laughed, and then Paul said, "I've got one that could be about that same fellow."

"All right," Curtis said. "Let's hear it."

"While the cashier in a restaurant was digging a man's change out of the cash register," Paul recounted, "the customer took a toothpick out of the little dispenser sitting on the counter, used it vigorously, and returned it to the container.

"'Now, see!' the customer said proudly to the cashier. 'I put it back. I'll bet you lose a heap o' money by people jest walkin' off with those picks!'"

Curtis and I groaned at that one.

"Well, I got another short one," said Curtis. "A boy about twelve years old was looking up admiringly at his tall father. 'Dad, do you think I'll ever grow another foot?' Before his dad could answer, his little sister, aged about five, spoke up: 'What d'ya want with another one? You got two big ones now!'"

August 30th

Cora Hunter has lived at FairAcres Home nearly as long as I have, and I thought I knew all of her best stories;

but somehow she'd never gotten around to telling me about Claude Hartley and his mail-order baby until yesterday. Esther and I were having tea in Cora's apartment, and the conversation (as it often does) meandered into the past. We were remembering wearing "middy blouses" when we were about nine and ten years old.

Cora said, "Those awful things! We pinned them over at the sides to try to make them fit." She illustrated the folding. "Remember?"

"No," said Esther. "I don't believe I wore those things."

"You'd remember if I showed you a picture… Wait a minute…"

Cora reached in the bottom drawer of her desk and brought out a battered photo album, and found a faded picture of herself and her sister, Louella, each holding the end of a jump rope and smiling self-consciously. They wore dark bloomers and white middy blouses with sailor collars.

"Bloomers!" we whooped. "Each leg full enough to hold a sack of potatoes! How could we ever jump rope in those things?"

On the same page was a picture of a pleasant-looking man, smiling and holding a large dog by a leash.

"Oh," said Cora, "there's Claude. I haven't thought of him in too long. Much too long for someone who was such a happy part of my childhood." She looked so very pensive that Esther and I were intrigued.

"Tell us about him," I suggested.

Cora filled up our cups, emptying the teapot. "When Louella and I were about five and six-and-a-half, we spent a lot of time next door with Claude and Fanny Hartley. They had no children and always seemed to be glad to see us. Claude would read us the funny papers. He could wiggle his ears and cross his eyes, which fascinated us.

"One day when we went over we found Claude sitting in his living room with a Sears Roebuck catalog open on his knees.

"'What are you ordering, Claude?' I asked. (He insisted we call him that, even though our parents thought it a bit forward.) Claude's eyes lit up with an idea that I am sure just that moment occurred to him.

"'I'm thinking about ordering a baby,' he said.

"'A baby?'

"'Un-huh. Don't you think that's a good idea?'

"We were entranced. We watched him print BABY BOY in the left-hand space of the order form.

"'Now, let's see… It says size. How big do you think he ought to be?'

"'Nine pounds!' Louella and I both cried. We had a new baby cousin who weighed nine pounds.

"NINE LBS, printed Claude.

"'Now, what color eyes?' We whispered together and decided on blue.

"'What color hair?' he asked. I said, 'red,' and Louella said, 'black.'

"Claude said, 'Let's compromise with brown.' And he printed BROWN. 'Now, let's see, do you suppose I should just put down ten fingers and ten toes?... No, I don't think so. That's understood. Do you think I dare ask for a good disposition? No, that's asking too much. We'll just have to hope for a sweet baby. You girls wish for us to have a sweet baby in your prayers, hear?'

"We did. Oh, we did. And after a few days we started watching for the postman. When we saw him leave a box at Claude's house one day, we went flying over. But, alas, it was just a part for his tractor. More days passed. Finally, we couldn't stand it any longer and we asked Claude about the delay.

"'Well, I'll tell you,' said Claude. 'Mr. Sears wrote me that there was a shortage of nine-pound boys, but he said he would put us one on back-order.'

"So we had to be patient. And one day there was a phone call, asking that the little girls come next door. We dashed over and found Claude and Fanny bending over a carriage that contained a baby boy—kicking and crowing.

"'It came!' we shouted.

"'It came!' said Claude, not telling us that the baby had come via an adoption from the county orphanage. Louella and I had always had a healthy respect for Mr.

Sears and Mr. Roebuck, who supplied us with clothes, underclothes, shoes, skates, and even pencil boxes; but after this event, our admiration knew no bounds.

"'He even has blue eyes and brown hair,' said Louella, 'like we ordered.'

"'Yeah, and I think they threw in a good disposition, too,' said Claude.

"And they did. He was a happy child and a fine son to his parents all of their lives.

"So, looking at Claude's kind face in the photo album these long years later, I want to tell him, 'You did good to get that fine boy, Claude. You couldn't have done better if you *had* ordered him.'"

Cora looked thoughtful. "You know," she said, "I think there should be a special reward in heaven for childless couples who befriend neighborhood children whose parents are too busy to give them much time. They fill a real need. I could never, ever forget Claude and Fanny Hartley. They took the time to listen to us and play with us. Dear people…I hope they knew how I loved them."

September 5th

One of our waitresses in the dining room is a songbird. She brightens many a morning for me as she carries my tray, humming an old tune in a sweet, unobtrusive voice.

One morning she was completely quiet. She smiled at me, but there was no soft tune coming from her throat.

"Don't you feel well this morning, Dorothy?" I asked.

"I'm all right, thank you, ma'am," she said.

But I wasn't. The dining room was too quiet. After a little investigating, I learned that a very proper resident had complained to the management, saying it was not good manners for a waitress to sing as she served us.

Phooey! Dorothy's *joie de vivre* just bubbled over into soft singing. Why stifle a bit of impulsive happiness? It was like killing a mockingbird.

Some of us ganged up and approached management. We assured them that Dorothy's soft humming and singing was anything but objectionable; that it was a boon to us, especially on dark mornings.

"Let our bird sing!" we told them.

And they did! This morning as I was placing a bowl of cornflakes on my tray, I heard a sweet, beloved tune from long ago being sung softly nearby: "Shall We Gather at the River?" Dorothy winked at me.

My coffee tasted better than it had in days.

September 10th

Tonight as we sat finishing our after-dinner coffee, Cecil pulled a small book from his pocket. It was a collection of humorous Southern stories.

"I want to read you-all something funny," he said. "Maybe some of you have heard it before, but it is worth hearing again." He read:

A young man named Jones, from "The Holy City" (that's Charleston, of course), went North to seek his fortune. He applied for work in Chicago, and the personnel manager of a large company there wrote to the Charleston person whose name had been given as a reference.

Back came a prompt and very polite answer, stating that the company would be indeed fortunate to obtain the services of the young man in question, because he was of impeccable ancestry, his mother having been a Ravenel, his great-grandfather on the maternal side a Rhett, and his grandmother on the paternal side a Pinckney.

The personnel manager replied, thanking the gentleman and saying, "Unfortunately, we want to hire Mr. Jones for clerical work, not for breeding purposes."

September 11th

This story was sent to me by a friend. It gave me such a laugh that I decided to repeat it to you, Dear Diary, in spite of its scandalousness. Forgive me, but I can't resist:

*I heard a sweet beloved tune from long ago being sung
softly nearby. Dorothy winked at me.*

It seems that the daughter of a new-rich man became engaged and desired a showy wedding. The indulgent father approached his friend Ralph, also of questionable background, but a forceful and productive man.

"I'll tell you what, Ralph," the father said, "you're a good manager. I want you to manage my daughter's weddin'."

When Ralph demurred, saying he didn't know any-thing about fancy hitchings, the father said, "There's nothin' to it. All you have to do is copy this weddin' I read about in the New York paper." He pulled a clipping from his pocket. This was in the days when weddings were extravaganzas and newspapers vied with each other for elaborate coverage. "Two Broadway stars got married, and they had a big to-do. I want you to copy this weddin' down to a T. It don't matter how much it costs. She's my only baby girl."

Ralph followed orders. The church was banked not with Southern smilax, but with orchids. Instead of organ music there was an orchestra. Instead of local talent ren-dering (rending?) "O Promise Me," "Because," and "I Love You Truly," there was an imported musical comedy star getting highly dramatic and emotional with Grieg's "*Ich Liebe Dich.*"

The wedding march started, and twelve bridesmaids carrying enormous bouquets, which trembled a little, walked singly and slowly down the aisle, and were met by twelve groomsmen who came in from the side. Then the orchestra leader gave a signal, and Lohengrin's familiar "March" crescendoed to signal the bride's entrance.

Just then a small boy appeared from nowhere and started running up and down the aisle, giggling and pinching all the women he could reach on their bosoms! He got out of the way as the startled bride and her red-faced father proceeded to the altar where the ceremony took place.

After the rites the infuriated father sought out Ralph. "Who let that crazy boy in? What in God's name was he doing? How could you let—"

"Hey, wait a minute there," said Ralph, taking the newspaper account out of his pocket. "You tole me t' copy this thing exactly, didn't yuh? Awright." He pointed to a line of print. "Look right here. Just read that. It says, 'As the bride and her father started down the aisle, a nervous titter ran through the audience.'"

Whoo-eee!

September 15th

We have a new resident on our hall: Annette Hollingsworth. Isn't that a pretty name, Dear Diary?

At first we were a little nervous about her. She seemed too "persnickety": every hair was always in its proper place, even at breakfast. She even wore heels and carried a lorgnette! The latter really got to us until we learned that her eyesight was failing, and she really needed the lorgnette to read the menu.

She's turned out to be natural and "fun." She entertained us this afternoon with a story she swears is true…and I believe her.

Marcia had invited Annette and Cora and me over. (She has a wonderful garden to which she has attracted many interesting birds, and it's always a pleasure to spend time there.) When we arrived, Marcia brought out iced tea with sprigs of her own mint, and we settled in the shade of the red trumpet creeper blooming on an arbor near her patio.

We were commiserating with Cora, who has a sore throat. Her trouble has affected her speech so that there is a hoarseness, a raspiness, to her voice.

"Have you seen a doctor about that?" asked Annette.

"No," was the reply. "I'm gargling with warm salt water. It will go away."

"I do hope so," said Annette. "I'd hate to think you might have to endure the drastic treatment I did. My symptoms sounded just like yours."

"What did you have?" croaked Cora.

"'Singer's Nodes,' the doctor called them. Bad irritations on the larynx."

"What did he do for you?" I asked, trying to keep Cora from talking.

"He put me on the 'Silence Cure.'"

"The Silence Cure? You mean you had to stop talking?" I asked incredulously.

"That I did. For three long months. Not a sound was I allowed to make with my voice. I couldn't even call the doctor an old meanie!"

"Annette, are you telling us that you couldn't utter a word for *three months?*" Marcia exclaimed.

"That's what I'm telling you," she said, and crossed her heart.

"How awful!" whispered Cora, putting her hand to her throat and looking worried.

"How unbelievable!" said our hostess.

"'Unspeakable' is the right word," said Annette wryly. "I went about clutching my pad and pencil for dear life, pointing at things, gesticulating, grimacing, feeling like a female Harpo Marx.

"My youngest child, Billy, told everybody, 'Th' doctor tol' Mama to shut up! She can't even holler at me!" He was the envy of his class.

"I was the talk of the town for a while. Howard told me that men hailed him on the street and asked how much he had paid Dr. Smoak for the prescription, and said they were going to send their wives to the same man."

We laughed. I could just hear Sam saying something like that with a twinkle in his eye.

"Yes. Everyone though it was a big joke," Annette continued. "But they should have to get three children dressed, fed, and off to school without uttering a sound."

"Good *heavens*," I said. "How did you *do* it?"

"Sometimes I wonder," said Annette. "There were a lot of frustrations. I hated having to listen to the telephone ring itself out and wonder who was on the other end. (This was long before answering machines.) And one of the worst things was going to a meeting and hearing something proposed that made you shiver with disapproval...and not be able to object."

We all nodded sympathetically.

"I was feeling quite sorry for myself after four weeks, when it came time to return to the doctor for a checkup. Of course, I secretly harbored hopes that my sentence would be lifted, but Dr. Smoak shook his head and said the growths were still in evidence. He warned me it might take even longer than three months!

"When I got home, Howard and the children could feel the strain and disappointment in the air, and reacted accordingly. Billy said, 'I wish you could yell at me again, Mama. Why don't you bless me out on that paper?' And he pointed to my ever-present yellow pad, which I was beginning to loathe."

Annette paused to drink some tea.

"The end of this story is that I was released from my

'vow of silence' by Dr. Smoak at the scheduled time, thank goodness. The nodules had disappeared, and I had learned some valuable lessons about 'logorrhea,' a ten-dollar word for talking too much. Overuse, the doctor explained, was the root cause of the condition."

There was appreciation all around for Annette's narrative, but Cora didn't say a word. She just smiled and clapped to express her appreciation of the tale and to show that it had had its intended effect.

This had been a sobering (as well as an entertaining) story, and we made Cora promise to go see the doctor tomorrow.

We sat quietly for a while, none of us speaking, just taking in the beauty of the garden. It was then that a shimmering green and red presence flitted in and out of the sunlight among the crimson blooms nearby. When the tiny creature flew away, Marcia, who has always been an avid birder as well as gardener, told us that it was a Ruby-Throated Hummingbird.

"You see," I declared, patting Cora's hand, "silence has its own rewards."

3

Let There Be Light

March 3rd

Dear Diary, I have not "kept you up on things" in so many months, but I am determined to start "telling all" again. This item I am a little ashamed to tell about, even to you, however. How dumb can you *get!*

The two lamps on one side of my living room would not come on today: a table lamp and a floor lamp. I had recently put in new bulbs, so I decided there must be something wrong with the electric wiring. This afternoon I reported my trouble to The Home's office.

In a few minutes two men from Maintenance arrived. They tested the lamps; then one of the men reached up to a switch on the wall, turned it, and the lamps flamed with light.

I was mortified. I had never bothered with that switch, preferring to turn the lamps on separately; but *somebody* had turned it off.

The men were nice about it. I suppose, working at FairAcres, they are used to Dumb Ol' Mixed-up Souls.

Then I had an idea. I said, "Just to keep your trip from being a complete waste of time, how about turning my mattress for me?" (The heavy double-bed mattress was awaiting fresh linens, and the housekeeper had said she could not turn it.)

Without a word, the two strong men readily gave the mattress an easy flip.

Afterward, they left politely. I'm sure the words, "What's next?" must have been doing through their minds.

March 7th

When I'm dating anything, I still find it so hard to write the year: 2000. I think I'm doing something wrong. It seems like science fiction.

Dear Sam used to say he was born in "oh-nine." Will children born this year have to say, "I was born in 'oh-oh'?"

March 11th

One of our residents, Eloise Courtland, taught first grade for thirty-two years (hardy soul). She told us a funny tale at lunch today. It happened once when she was teaching the Pledge of Allegiance to her students.

She told them to put their right hands over their hearts. All the children put their hands over their hearts except for little Susie, who put her little right hand over her little right buttock.

"Susie! I said to put your hand over your heart!"

"This is my heart."

"What makes you think so?"

"Well, whenever my grandmother comes around, she pats me, right here, and says, 'Bless your little heart!'"

April 7th

A choice crowd just happened to gather this afternoon in the Country Store. Some came for coffee, some for things like toothpaste and Kleenex, and some just for company.

We talked for a while about Katie Parsons, who died last night in the Health Care Center (still the Infirmary to me). Katie (short for Katrina) was a great old gal. She volunteered for everything—she played the kazoo in our kitchen band, and sang soprano in the quartet.

That led us to the subject of our chaplain, who will now have to conduct another funeral. Poor man. Never any infant baptisms, seldom any weddings—just the funerals. He must get tired of flattering the deceased and comforting the bereaved.

April 15th

T. S. Eliot wrote a poem that begins, "April is the cruelest month," and now that we have reached this day—the fifteenth—I agree with him. All the Poor Old Souls here at The Home are scurrying around finishing (with each other's help) the filling out of the complicated tax returns and dropping them in the box before the mailman comes.

I dispatched my envelope, too, but with no glee. I would not begrudge Uncle Sam his share if he were not so wasteful. But since he is wanton in that respect—pouring money down rat holes, and throwing my hard-earned money away in absurd, almost obscene, ways, I take no joy in making out the check and mailing it.

Not only does the White House seem not so snowy white to me any more, but the whole city of Washington, which should be beautiful, has a kind of unattractive, sleazy atmosphere, to my mind, and I don't like that.

April 19th

When the ladies' talk here turns to bathing, I clam up; and if their baths or showers are modified by the word "daily," I retreat even further. I meet my "water-loo" twice a week, and I dread each encounter a little more than the last. There is mortal danger involved.

Dear Diary, you might ask, "If a tub bath is so dangerous, why don't you take a shower?"

Alas, the shower is a knob hanging over the tub. I still have to climb over the side, which seems ten feet high when your poor knee joints don't bend properly.

The whole time I am soaping and rinsing, I'm worrying about getting out. When I finally get my poor old slippery self hoisted across the high side and safely on the bathmat, I could cry with relief. I feel like going back to bed and resting for a few hours.

Sometimes I send up a fervent prayer, something like: "Lord, please take your eye off that sparrow for a minute, and help get this poor old wet 'creature' out of this tub, unbroken." Praise be, He does. I don't think I could manage it by myself.

I don't know how many times I heard my parents and grandparents say, "Cleanliness is next to Godliness" (and I said it to my own brood). But these days, Dear Diary, cleanliness seems next to impossible!

April 25th

I dropped into the library after lunch today and saw several people absorbed in watching two men sitting at a small table flipping rounds of plastic into a glass cup. It was Paul and Curtis, playing Tiddledywinks!

When Paul looked up and saw my astonished look, he said, "Why not? It sure beats staying home and watching *General Hospital* on TV."

He bore down on an edge of plastic and sent it sailing into the cup. Satisfying sound.

As I walked to my apartment I decided I would get somebody to buy me a Parcheesi game and put it in the library. Playing that with somebody would be better than playing endless games of solitaire.

April 27th

Today is a boring day. Our Program Director is on vacation—no movie, no sing-along, no Bible study, no bird walk—not even bingo.

I suppose I will get out my special notebook and write a poem.... Maybe I will write an ode to the Vidalia onion.

What I would really like to write, if I felt equal to it, is a tribute to the Founding Fathers of our country—those men who labored through endless, uncomfortable days in Philadelphia, away from their families and their work, to bring forth not just a raw, new nation, but one shaped and bounded, ruled and regulated, strong and secure in its breathtakingly new concept and power.

How unbelievably lucky we were and are, that God blessed us with those men, at that time, who were able to accomplish such a phenomenal feat!

I remember what Winston Churchill said of the gallant R.A.F. flyers in World War II: "Never in the field of human conflict was so much owed by so many to so few."

Oh, to have Churchill's tongue and wit, to conjure up a phrase to describe what we owe to our Founders. God bless their memory, and keep it bright.

April 28th

So much for my "boring day," Dear Diary. There was a big to-do here last night for your typical retirement home. About nine o'clock a police car came to a screeching halt under the *porte cochère,* and four police officers piled out. They raced into the office just off the lobby and confronted Allen Stimson, our night clerk.

"Where does Mrs. Tinken live?" they demanded of Allen.

As his fingers raced through The Home's directory, he asked, "What has she done?"

"We don't know. She just called 911 and said she was having some kind of trouble."

"She's in room 332-C," yelled Allen. "Follow me."

They raced down Main Hall to C Hall rooms and banged on Geneva's door. She opened it and stood looking astonished in her bathrobe and hair curlers.

"What in the world—?"

"What's your trouble, Mrs. Tinken?" one of the officers asked.

"Trouble?"

"You told the operator you were having some kind of trouble—"

Geneva put her hands on her hips and snorted. "I told him I was having trouble with my Boulangerie watch. I just wanted to know what time it was."

Did I call it a typical retirement home? Well, I guess you could say it's typical if other homes have a Geneva Tinken enrolled!

May 1st

I took a short walk today on our campus and saw a rainbow!

I've always had a "thing" about rainbows. They're not just curves of colors in the sky, they're miracles! My younger son, Raymond, knew how much I loved the beautiful arcs, and sometimes he would come running into the house, yelling, "Mama! Rainbow!" We would dash out to the backyard and gaze at that glorious wonder in the sky. Once we were thrilled to see two gorgeous curves, and a faint touch of color that looked like it was trying to be a third!

> My heart leaps up when I behold
> A rainbow in the sky....

The poet said it so well. I can be feeling weary and dull and hopeless, and suddenly see that miracle in the sky—those heavenly colors—bending, and I take on a new fervor for life. A world where such a vision can hover over us can't be all bad.

Later

At supper tonight we talked about the rainbow and about the fact that today is May Day.

"I never hear any mention of May Day the way we grew up with it," commented Retta.

"I think the Russians ruined May Day," said Sidney. "When they were the Soviet Union, they had a big military parade on May Day, didn't they? I seem to remember seeing news broadcasts with Nikita Khrushchev and a lot of other somber men in overcoats watching as rows and rows of tanks and missiles and soldiers marched by."

"That's right," agreed Christine, "but flowers and dancing were what I always associated with May Day. When I was in elementary school, I looked forward to the May Day party all year. I was overjoyed when I finally was chosen to be in the group that danced around the maypole."

"Oh, we had a maypole!" I remembered. "Weren't you a 'May Princess' when you got to be in the dance, Christine? Tell us about it."

"We didn't have a real maypole, but our teacher— Mrs. Lemon was her name—rigged up one of those long poles they used to open and close the windows in the schoolrooms...the ones that were too high to reach."

"Oh, I remember those!" someone else exclaimed.

Christine continued. "She and the custodian had a time getting the pole anchored out in the playground. I think it had rained a lot that spring. Anyway, they finally got it upright, and it looked beautiful. Mrs. Lemon had attached long, pastel ribbons to the top, and they fluttered in the breeze. I think they were made of crepe paper.

"Well, all the May princesses, including me, had practiced our dance well. We were carefully winding our streamers around the pole, ducking under or crossing over each other at precise times, when the girl in front of me looked up just in time to see the pole listing toward her in slow motion.

"'Timm-berrrrr!' she yelled, and we shrieked and dispersed in all directions. It seemed awful at the time," laughed Christine, "but now it is funny to remember."

When I got back to my apartment tonight I looked up the William Wordsworth poem about the rainbow:

> My heart leaps up when I behold
> A rainbow in the sky;
> So it was when my life began;
> So is it now I am a man;
> So be it when I shall grow old,
> Or let me die!

The Child is father of the Man;
I could wish my days to be
Bound each to each by natural piety.

Sentiments I still share with the poet after these many, many days since I was a child.

May 5th

At breakfast this morning I was told that Marie Welborn was being sent to the infirmary. On my way back to my apartment I stopped at her room. "Come in," she called faintly, at my knock. She was sitting in her lounge chair looking even smaller and more birdlike than usual.

"Oh, Hattie!" she said. "I was *hoping* you'd come."

Marie doesn't have a lot of friends here. I think many people consider her too quiet and rather inconsequential, but I know her worth. She taught all of my children in the sixth grade.

That's an important grade, to my mind. Children are becoming aware of a host of things and are easily confused. Marie had gone out of her way to try to steer them right. I was grateful to her.

She pointed to an open suitcase on the bed.

"They are coming for me in a few minutes. I have a feeling I might not see this room again. They told me just to pack nightgowns and a bathrobe; but, oh, Hattie, there's something else I want to take. Would you please get that white box off of the shelf of my closet?" She pointed.

I did. The box was about three inches wide and two feet long. I put it in her lap and she opened it.

Inside was a straight razor, a round soap brush, and an old folded black leather strap. "Strop" my father had called his.

"Papa would sharpen this razor on that strap every morning," said Marie. "I would sit on a little footstool in the bathroom and watch him."

Marie's eyes filled with tears. "It probably seems silly, Hattie, but everything about him was so important to me. My mother was an invalid, with no time or strength for me. I didn't have any brothers or sisters. My dear father was my whole life. When he finished shaving, he would pick me up and hold my cheek against his. He smelled so good." She picked up the soap brush. "I think I can still smell him. He meant so terribly much in my life…I need something of him now, close to me…. Do you think?…"

"Don't worry, Marie. I will take the box, and bring it to you later. I'll help you find a hiding place for it, if necessary."

Her face brightened, "And thank you for not thinking me an old sentimental fool. You see, he was the only man in my life…."

Inside the box was a straight razor, a soap brush,
and an old black leather strap.

I hugged her and left the room, carrying her beloved box and trying to hold back the tears until I could get to my own nest. I was consumed with pity for that special little woman who had led a good, useful life, instructing other women's children, with so little reward. Life is not fair; that's "for sure."

May 7th

A memory:

My dear grandmother never said, "Hurry up." She always said, "Make haste, child. Make haste!"

I used to wonder what "makase, makase" meant, but in my grandmother's soft voice it sounded better than "Hurry up!"

May 8th

I visited Marie late this afternoon and took her precious box to her. It was wonderful to see her face light up, especially because she seems so weak. I tucked the box close to her side with her hand resting on it and sat with her for just a few minutes. When I left, the nurse assured me Marie could keep her treasures right where they would comfort her.

As I was returning to the main building, I found myself walking with Eloise.

"Hattie," she said, "I've been thinking off and on all day about the story you told us at breakfast."

"Oh, my!" I said, a bit startled. "What story was that?" (After all, breakfast had been more than eight hours ago.)

"The one about the 'birthday door,'" she said.

Then I remembered. We had been talking about how hard it had been to give up our homes. At least, hard for most of us.

"Not for me," said Ralph. "I couldn't wait to kiss that old place good-bye. The roof leaked and the grass grew three inches a day, and I was too wobbly to stand on a chair and put in a lightbulb."

"And I remember I would forget to put the garbage out—so it piled up—and smelled," added Sarah.

There were sympathetic nods around the table.

After a minute I said, "Even so, I found it terribly hard to let go of the place we called 'home' for forty-four years. I especially hated to part with our den door. It had treasured markings on the back.

"I'm sure I've told some of you about it before. On each child's birthday, Sam would stand the child up to that door and mark the top of his or her head and would write the initials and the date. There was great anticipation of the measuring to see how much the child had grown in a year. We called it 'the birthday tree' door—and you can imagine how I hated to leave it. I knew it would disappear under a fresh coat of (very needed) paint.

"But I got such a nice surprise several weeks after I

moved here. When the man (a stranger) who bought my house got ready to paint that door, he took the time to take a photograph of it and sent it, carefully wrapped, to me!"

"What a considerate gesture," said Eloise that night when she spoke to me. "I've been thinking off and on all day about the kindness and thoughtfulness of that nice man! Chivalry is not dead!"

And I suppose it's not. Not *completely.*

May 12th

Ella McRae came to FairAcres several months ago. She says she likes it very much, except for one thing: There is a large lamppost just outside her bedroom window. It bears a light that comes on at dusk and goes off at dawn. Ella draws her draperies, but says the light is still so strong that she can't sleep.

She appealed to our administrator, Mr. Detwiler. He called the power company and asked them to move the lamp. They promised to do so, but after a month of waiting he had to call them again. Nothing happened.

Ella was getting frantic and looking quite "peak-ed" from sleeplessness.

"I never liked a light on anywhere near my bed," she told us. "And now, in my old age, I have one glaring at me all night!"

Somebody suggested that she call Maintenance and get hold of our prime "fixer" Arthur Priest. Ella appealed to him and that very night, about eleven o'clock, Arthur came to the section of the building in front of Ella's apartment, located the lamp, took his B-B gun, and shot out the light.

That was a month ago. Nothing has been heard from the police or the power company. Ella says she is sleeping the nights through now, in "blissful darkness!"

4

Goings and Comings

May 19th

I went to the Health Care Center several more times to see Marie, but her worsening condition had affected her mind, and I'm not sure that she knew me. I was relieved to hear that she had gone to her rest. Her memorial service was this afternoon, and as I sat in the chapel I wondered what had happened to her father's shaving outfit. One of the nurses told me that she had the little shaving brush in her hand when she died. I hope it went into the ground with her.

Later

Two more friends gone—Marie and, back in April, Katrina. I'm thankful for both of them. Of course, I knew

Marie for many, many years, ever since my eldest child entered "Miss Welborn's" sixth-grade classroom. Just from teaching my three, she earned many stars in her crown, and I'm sure her legacy has spread far and wide.

Katrina—Katie—had lived here about two years; yet I felt as if I had known her for much longer. She was one of those engaging, positive-thinking people who add a lot to our community at The Home. I can still see her playing that kazoo.

May 25th

Marybelle is one of our most popular waitresses. Her sunny smile is a tonic on dark mornings. Therefore, we were worried this morning when Marybelle was not smiling. Someone asked, "Aren't you well, dear?"

Marybelle rubbed her eyes with the back of her hand.

"I'm all right," she said, refilling Sidney's coffee cup, "but something bad happened last night."

"What?" we all asked, in chorus.

"My sister's house caught fire and burned down. To the ground."

There were many distressed reactions and general relief when we determined that there had been no loss of life. The family had returned home from a church dinner to find the flames already engulfing their residence.

Marybelle lowered her voice. "My sister and her husband

and their two children have moved in with us. Stan and I have three kids…and a small house." She wiped away a tear.

We all made sounds of commiseration.

As she took away a tray of plates we looked at each other and shook our heads. Poor girl. Poor children. Poor family.

May 30th

We have all, of course, been keeping up with Marybelle and her sister and the story of the fire. It turns out that old, faulty wiring was the cause of the blaze, and, unfortunately, their landlord had no insurance and says he is not going to rebuild the house.

Everyone was so crowded in Marybelle's house that they came up with a plan over the weekend to ease the strain. Marybelle's sister, Melinda, and her husband, Mike Hogan, and the baby moved back to Marybelle and Melinda's parents' house, about ten miles out in the country from Drayton. Six-year-old Lindy, who goes to the same school as Marybelle's children, is staying with her aunt and uncle in town, at least until school is out next month.

There has already been some talk at The Home about taking up a collection to help with replacing clothes and household goods.

June 3rd

My friend Marcia had a rather scary experience over Memorial Day. She flew to Cincinnati for a granddaughter's wedding. Coming back, she had to change planes in Charlotte. (We Southerners are convinced that when we die, we will have to change planes in Charlotte or Atlanta to go to Heaven or The Other Place.) This is the way Marcia told it to me.

"It was raining when the plane left Charlotte that night, but not terribly hard. However, in about twenty minutes the gentle rain turned into a really fierce storm. Lightning and thunder shook the plane with a vengeance.

"When we got over Charleston, the pilot's voice came over the intercom.

"'Folks, I'm sorry to tell you that we can't see the runway. We'll have to circle a while until the storm lets up. Bear with me.'

"We circled and circled. I was sitting by a window, but between the lightning flashes all I could see was blackness, and hateful gusts of rain dashing against the window glass. Twenty minutes…twenty-eight minutes… thirty-two minutes. I don't know much about aeronautics, but I know that a plane's supply of gas is not endless!

"I looked out once more. Not one tiny twinkling light could I see; just pounding rain.

"I turned to the man sitting by me. 'Is this getting a little bit scary?' I asked him.

"'I didn't think so until about five minutes ago,' he said. 'Now I find myself sitting here wishing I had been better to my little brother!'

"'Where else could we go to land?' I asked him.

"'I've been thinking about that,' he said. 'Columbia? Savannah? They're both probably as socked-in by this storm as Charleston is.'

"We were quiet for a moment.

"'Ma'am, do you mind telling me how old you are?'

"'I'm eighty-eight,' I told him.

"'Well, don't you worry, ma'am. That nice pilot's gonna get you down...'

"And just then the nice pilot's voice boomed over the intercom. 'Folks,' he said, 'we've just enough gas left to get back to Charlotte, and I'm goin'! They tell me I can see to land there—so—keep buckled up. Here we go!'

"The plane took an upward turn, and we clapped and shouted.

"We landed safely, spent a few hours in the Charlotte airport, and at daybreak another pilot flew us safely to Charleston."

"Marcia, were you very nervous?" I asked her.

"Nervous, nothin'! I was scared stiff... But do you know something, Hattie? Now when I think about that night, what I seem to remember best is the odd look on that man's face when he said, 'I'm sitting here wishing I had been better to my little brother.'"

June 17th

This morning after breakfast, some of us were sitting in the gazebo near the duck pond and talking about the circumstances of Marybelle's family when Sidney and Retta came up with a wonderful idea. The two conferred quietly, and then Sidney asked, "Is there a Habitat for Humanity affiliate in Drayton? Does anybody know?"

Nobody knew, but Sidney felt sure there would be such an office in this nice community—and it turns out that there is. Before the day was out, Sidney and Retta had driven over and gotten the paperwork required for the Habitat application process.

June 22nd

Today, Sidney and Retta took the Hogans to the Habitat affiliate, where they turned in their application, learned about the Habitat program, and looked at various house plans. Now we have to wait and see if the Selection Committee approves them, which usually takes at least several months.

July 18th

Every summer as a child I visited my grandparents in their small hometown in Alabama. It was heaven.

There were cousins visiting, too, and we filled the warm days and "stilly" nights with merriment—and devilment—that I love to remember.

A middle-aged or slightly older couple lived across the street—Mr. and Mrs. Harmon. Mr. Harmon had a small farm. Mrs. Harmon was a quiet little woman. We would see her occasionally, feeding her chickens or hanging out her washing. They had no children and, apparently, few friends.

After supper we would play in the quiet street, as long as we could see: games like hopscotch or tag or hide-and-seek. There was little traffic on that road.

Mr. and Mrs. Harmon would sit in their rocking chairs on their porch. I could see them silhouetted by the one-bulb light in their hallway. They would sit in utter silence. I remember thinking, even at age ten, that theirs was a dull existence.

Finally, at just about eight-thirty every night, Mr. Harmon would start yawning. I never had heard such loud yawns. Then he would stand up, stretch, yawn again, and say, "Time to undo, I reck'n," and they would go in the house and shut the door.

Mrs. Harmon was a sweet-looking woman. I hate to think how bored she must have been, how bleak her days and nights were. Today, she would probably rush through her chores so as not to miss a minute of her exciting soap opera. Or she might have looked at daytime shows that would have taught her some simple arts and crafts. At night the two of them could do a little mild betting on a Braves baseball game or listen joyfully to Lawrence Welk (still playing!). How much less dull and bleak the sum of their days would have been.... They wouldn't have had to "undo" nearly as early.... Poor things.

August 10th

I listened in on Paul and Curtis again tonight as they carried on their leisurely conversation. They talked about Luther Rigbe, whose wife died last month.

"Luther is surely gonna miss that lady," said Curtis. "She pushed him all over the place in that wheelchair. Do you think your wife would have done that for you, Paul?"

"Lord, no!" said Paul.

I never knew his wife, so I don't have any idea why he was so emphatic.

"My Eunice would have pushed me," said Curtis, "but I wouldn't have liked it. Eunice was a good old gal. She'd even scrub my back."

"She *would?*" asked Paul incredulously.

"She sure would. There's a place just beneath my shoulder blades that I can't reach with the soap. I'd yell for Eunice, and she would come and scour me good... I sure do miss that. I have a long-handled brush now, but it's not the same."

They were quiet after that, and I gave up on them and came home. The back-scrubbing talk had brought back some memories to me. Like Curtis, I have a long-handled brush, but I agree with him—it's not the same.

August 29th

Dear Diary, what a story I learned about this morning. Paul Chapin and Mr. Cruickshank approached me as I finished breakfast and asked to talk to me "in private." (That alone will probably start some tongues wagging.) There seemed to be people in every nook and cranny downstairs, so the three of us eventually had to return to my apartment. (Now the "Waggers" will have a field day!)

It seems that last night Mr. Cruickshank (hereinafter to be called Mr. C. because his name is too long) returned from supper to his cottage on the back of our campus and went into his second bedroom (which he had turned into a den, after his wife's death). As he tells it, he "nearly jumped out of my skin" when he discovered a large, male figure lying on his sofa, sound asleep.

Seeing the tousled blond hair and the rounded young cheeks, he realized it was the figure of an overgrown boy, and he shook him awake. The boy sat up, startled and frightened.

Mr. C. said, "Don't be scared, son." He told us that all the while he was thinking, *I'm the one who ought to be scared. He's twice as big as me.* (Mr. C. is a little man.)

Anyway, he soon got it out of the large intruder that his name was Perry Bagwell, that he was sixteen, and that he had run away from the McDonald Correctional Center in Monck's Corner.

"You walked all the way here? That's twenty miles!" Mr. C. exclaimed.

"Yes, sir. And I'm beat. When I found your back door unlocked and saw that sofa, I gave up."

Mr. C. explained that he was in a quandary about what to do, so he did what I would have done. He went to the phone and called Paul Chapin.

Paul went over immediately, and he and Mr. C. talked to the boy while Perry ate a huge peanut butter sandwich Mr. C. had fixed for him and drank several glasses of milk.

Both men told me that they couldn't believe he was in any really bad trouble. He had too nice a look in his eyes. There was more goodness than anything else in his young face, they assured me.

"What made you run away?" Mr. C. asked the boy.

"Mostly because I can't stand to be penned up," he said. "Then, too, they put me in a woodwork class. I'm no good at woodwork. I wanted to be in computers, but they said the computer class was full.... Also, I had a fight with my roommate. He was always wearing my clothes, and messing them up.... Yesterday, I broke one of the electric tools in class and got bawled out. Early this morning when they sent me to the storage house for something, I found a gate that hadn't been locked and I just walked out." He hung his head sheepishly.

Paul said, "I used to live in Monck's Corner, Perry. I believe I know the head man at that center—"

"Mr. Crawford? You know him?" Perry looked up.

"Slightly. He might remember me. I think I'll have to call him now. I'm sure they've got people out looking for you."

Paul told me the boy looked crestfallen.

"Do you have to?"

"I'm afraid so," Paul told him, looking him right in the eye kindly, but firmly. "I'm going to try to find some ways to help you, Perry, after you get back, but you'll have to return. Otherwise you're going to be in big trouble."

Paul said he knew Perry was "all right" because the boy looked him back in the eye and didn't argue and sat quietly.

Paul called the Center. The superintendent did remember him, and said, "Thank God, Paul. We've had search parties out all over the county looking for that boy."

"Could we keep him here tonight and bring him back in the morning? He's really beat."

"No, indeed. We must have him tonight. I'll send a van."

"How about letting me bring him?" Paul asked. "I'd like to have a chance to get to know the boy better."

"Thank you for the offer, but, no. I'll send my officers immediately. In fact, I'll call your local police and have them pick him up and hold him until we get there."

Well, Paul did not want the entire campus in an uproar over police cars arriving. He told me he got a promise from Perry that there would be no trouble and convinced Mr. Crawford to let the boy wait in the cottage with them. By the time the van arrived, Paul and Mr. C. had promised to come and visit and to put in a good word for the youngster with the superintendent.

"Hattie," Paul continued, "I wanted to talk with you about the whole thing before word gets out because some people are bound to be upset when they find out a runaway from the reformatory got into one of the cottages. I think you can reassure them—especially the ladies—better than we can. Also, you can help convince Mr. Detwiler not to file any charges over the incident."

"I want to help Perry," Mr. C. broke in. "I know he's not dangerous."

"I agree," said Paul. "Would you be willing to go with us tomorrow to visit the boy? I want you to see him for yourself. I'd really like to have you there, Hattie," he added, and my heart swelled. That Paul.

I told them I would be delighted to help.

5

A Boy in Trouble

August 30th

Our trip to Monck's Corner today went very well, but I am too tired tonight to tell you all that we learned, Dear Diary. I'll try to get a good night's sleep, and perhaps I'll have enough energy tomorrow to "fill you in" on all the details.

August 31st

Yesterday Paul and Roy (Mr. C.) and I drove to the Correctional Center and first met with Superintendent Crawford in his office. Mr. Crawford seemed sympathetic to his young charge and told us that Perry had not been in any real trouble at the facility until he ran away. The superintendent also welcomed our help. He told us that, in his many years of experience, he had found the very best thing for a youngster who had gotten into trouble was for a responsible adult to take an interest in helping the boy or girl.

After cautioning us not to make any promises to Perry, Mr. Crawford sent for the boy and left us alone to hear his story and get to know him.

In answer to our questions, Perry told us that his father had absconded years ago, when he (Perry) was about three. His mother had worked at various jobs. Two years ago, when she was working packing peaches at an orchard not too far from Leesburg, she had run away with a professional fruit-picker from Florida. Perry had moved in with her sister, "but she has four kids, and I jest crowded 'em up."

"Why were you sent to the Correctional Center?" Paul asked.

"You wouldn't believe my story," the boy said. "Nobody does."

"Try us," said Mr. C.

"Well, there was this boy—Miller Schofield. We had been in the same grade all through school. His family had a real nice house, and I used to like to go there. We'd study, and then we'd play Ping-Pong, and sometimes his mother would even invite me to stay for supper.

"One night a horn blew and blew in front of my aunt's house. I went out, and there was Miller in his father's brand new Volvo.

"Miller was wavin' his arm at me to get in the car. 'Dad and Mom went next door to play bridge,' he told me, 'and I slipped the car out of the garage. Come on. Jump in!' He patted the seat by him.

"'I didn't know you could drive,' I said.

"'I can't get a license 'til I'm sixteen, next month, but I can drive. Anybody could drive this thing! Come on!'

"I got in, and we roared off. The streets were kinda quiet—it was supper time—and Miller managed to get us out to the highway. We headed south, and he put his foot on the accelerator—50, 60, 70 miles an hour. When he got it up to 75, I was shakin', and beggin' him to slow down. He jest grinned at me; and the first thing you know, on a curve he lost control and we left the road and slammed into a telephone pole. My shoulder hit the dashboard. I heard Miller yell, 'Let's get out of here! This thing might catch fire!'

"Well, it didn't, but that Volvo was totaled. Completely smashed.

"We crawled out, and pretty soon some people came along and took us to the hospital. I had a dislocated shoulder, and Miller's knee had been cut on something. When you looked at that car, you could sure see we were lucky!

"I believe it was the telephone company that brought charges. We had wrecked one of their poles." He paused.

"Here's the bad part. At the hearing, Miller claimed that I was driving and that I had persuaded him to 'steal' the car. I denied it with all my might, but they believed him—probably because his dad is a big shot in town. Even my aunt didn't believe me. Three days later I was sent to the Center."

On the drive back from Monck's Corner, the three of us discussed Perry's situation.

"Hattie," said Paul, "I felt so sorry listening to that kid. I could hardly stand it. He had nobody to advise him or even to say a good word for him. He didn't have a chance."

"I have to find a way to help this young fellow," said Mr. C.

"Oh, I do hope you can!" I said fervently. "What do you think we can do?"

"Well," Paul said thoughtfully, "Mr. Crawford said he would welcome our interest. What I'd really like to do is get the case reopened. I want to make that lying young scoundrel, Miller Schofield, eat dirt."

"I'd like to be there to see you do it," I said.

Paul drove silently for a few minutes. "At the very least, I would like to have Perry back to visit us. As soon as his time of punishment is over—for running away—I would like to bring him to The Home on a Sunday for dinner."

We are all going to think about what we can do, and Paul said he will call Mr. Crawford. I agreed to talk to Mr. Detwiler about the situation and help to calm any fears among the residents if word gets out that Perry is from the Correctional Center.

September 26th

Right after our trip to Monck's Corner, Paul Chapin caught a terrible cold that ended up in a bad cough. He wasn't able to do anything about Perry Bagwell for three weeks.

Meanwhile, Mr. C. had helped out by learning the name of a good lawyer in Leesburg through a friend of his late wife's, who had lived there.

Finally, when Paul was better, he called the lawyer and discussed Perry's case.

Yesterday, Paul drove to Leesburg, about two hours away, and proceeded to the Schofield home, after getting directions. School was out, and Miller was at home.

None of us knows what exactly transpired, or how he did it, but Paul got a confession out of that scared boy. I hope some day Paul will break down and tell me what happened. Anyway, he put Miller in his car, drove to Mr. Schofield's office, and had the boy repeat his confession to his father.

Before the day was over, Miller Schofield admitted, before his father, Paul, Paul's lawyer, and a telephone company official, that it had been his idea to take the car out, not Perry's, and that he had been driving.

Next, Paul and the lawyer contacted the judge who had heard the case. The judge was chagrinned.

"I don't like for mistakes to be made in my court," he told Paul, and he promised to get the whole mess straightened out quickly.

Paul said he couldn't help feeling sorry for Miller Schofield's parents; but he felt no sympathy at all for the whimpering Miller.

October 4th

Musing.

Dear Diary, who shall I vote for in November to lead our wonderful land? Mr. Bush or Mr. Gore? They both seem to be nice, good-looking young (to me) men— equally qualified. How to choose?

I think I will write the same letter to both of them asking what, if anything, they plan to do about my pet peeve: that super-loud, ugly background "music" on television, the hateful sound that drowns out the players' lines and absolutely spoils so much entertainment for me.

October 18th

Good news today. Perry has been released from the Center. He returned to Leesburg, to his aunt's, but Paul says that the court will have to rule on a guardian for him if they can't find his mother.

Paul and Mr. Cruickshank plan to bring Perry to The Home to visit one weekend soon.

October 20th

Christine was feeding the ducks when I happened by the pond this afternoon. It was growing very chilly outside, so I asked her to come to my apartment for a cup of coffee and a piece of cake. We were talking about the weather, when she became pensive.

"I just don't like cold weather very much…makes me miss Florida," she said. "Fall's a sad, sad season, I think. Don't you think so? It seems like everything is dying."

We reached my front door. "Come in," I said. "I'll tell you how I feel about the colder season when I read you a poem I wrote last night. If you can call my amateur versifying poetry." After we had settled down with our refreshments, I took my notebook out of the desk and read her these lines.

THE SOFTNESS OF AUTUMN

Some people say that Autumn
Is a woeful time, a dying.
But I—I take special heart
When crimson leaves start flying.

There's a gentleness, a softness
That's assuaging to the soul.
I hear a haunting melody—
A song—a barcarole.

I want to run and sing and dance
Even though I'm sober.
I only know that I'm a better
Person in October.

Christine was quiet a minute and said, "I don't call that amateurish versification. It would make a good song. What did you say the title was?"

"I called it 'The Softness of Autumn.'"

"Well, I'll try to have a whole new idea about autumn now, Hattie. I'm grateful to you for lifting my spirits."

October 30th

Paul and Mr. C. had Perry to Sunday dinner here and then took him to see the beach.

"You should have seen his face," Paul reported. "He had never seen the ocean...."

On the drive back to Leesburg, Paul said, Perry was very quiet.

"What's the matter?" asked Paul.

"Well, sir, I'm just wonderin' what to do now they've let me out of the Center." Perry went on to admit that things were not going well in Leesburg. He wasn't happy to be back in school with Miller, and his aunt didn't seem too pleased at the idea of becoming his official guardian.

"How would you like to come to Drayton…be a guest at my cottage for a while?"

Paul said the boy's face lit up. "I'd like that fine!"

"It can just be temporary. I'll have to contact the court and your aunt. But if you want me to, I'd like to explore getting you placed with a nice family in Drayton. Also, we'll have to see about transferring you right away to the town's high school. If you need a little tutoring, Mr. Cruickshank and I can help you."

"That would be great!" said Perry enthusiastically.

Paul said it was good to see how pleased Perry was that somebody was taking charge of his life, and turning it in the right direction.

"Maybe I'm being too bossy, Hattie," Paul said, frowning. "What makes me think I'm the right one, at my age, to take over a young boy's life?"

"*Who better?*" I asked, and meant it.

November 3rd

This is a wonderful place to live when you're beginning to fall apart. My fellow residents keep good tabs on me. They've heard me say that I put on lipstick by dead reckoning. So they tell me when some of it has landed on the tip of my nose.

I can't see the part in my hair anymore. I have to comb my hair "by ear" (from memory). Sometimes there's a hunk of it on the east side of my head that belongs on the west. Nice people stop me and straighten it. They even tell me when I'm wearing mismatched shoes or earrings.

The more my eyesight fails, the more I appreciate what a wonderful place this retirement home is. Not only the staff, but the residents are looking out for the "Poor Old Soul" (as Sam used to call me affectionately when I complained about some frustration or other). They steer me to the right door; they read my mail to me; they carry my tray in the dining room; they watch out for spots on my clothes—and they tell me kindly. I thank the Lord every single night for their goodness.

And now my hearing is going, too. I have hearing aids, which roar and cut up sometimes, and help sometimes. But I'm missing a lot of "good stuff." Someone may have to supply me with a tin cup and pencils!

November 7th

Mr. C. took several of us to the elementary school to vote on Tuesday. On the way home he said, "I'm not fortunate enough to have children of my own, but it's funny: two boys have taken up with me in my old age. One was Cliffie, Arthur Priest's nice little son who helped me dig in my garden, and who unearthed some rare bottles." (I wrote you about that happening, Dear Diary.) "He and I are still great friends. And now this fine young fellow, Perry Bagwell, lands on my sofa, of all places! I guess I'm just lucky."

They're the lucky ones, Mr. C., I thought. He's one fine gentleman.

November 9th

A memory.

The Great Depression was still on when Sam and I got married. In the ceremony, when Sam said to me, "With all my worldly goods I thee endow," his father snorted out loud! He knew that Sam didn't have worldly good number one to bestow on me...or anyone else.

Later in the evening, on our "wedding trip" (two days in Beaufort, South Carolina), we stopped at a roadside restaurant to get something to eat. (Neither of us had tasted a crumb of the good refreshments at our wedding.) Sam leaned over to look at the menu, and a number of grains of rice fell from his thick hair and clattered onto the hard table top. I guess it sounded as loud as gunshots to us nervous newlyweds, and several people around us giggled. Sam flushed and said, "Come on, Hattie, let's get out of here."

A funny start to forty-four wonderful years.

<u>6</u>

Antiques

November 10th

Paul told me tonight that he and Curtis were sitting on the terrace this afternoon "shooting the breeze" (for once I had not been listening) when they saw something so strange coming down the driveway they could hardly believe their eyes.

"Hattie, it looked like a big yellow insect," Paul said, "except that it wasn't crawling. It was going about twenty miles an hour. We stood up to watch as it eased under the *porte cochère* and stopped. We could see Hazel and the Hendersons sitting on the front porch, and you should have seen their expressions when that apparition rolled up and a nice-looking young man hopped out, smiling.

"Of course, we had to go over and check things out, and he turned out to be Al McNaughton, the son of Allen and Alicia McNaughton. You know, Hattie, that pleasant couple from Orangeburg. Allen's a nice fellow.

"Well, son Al told us the car was a 1937 Cord Special roadster that he had just bought in Atlanta. He had had it shipped by truck to Orangeburg, so this was his first long trip. Fifty miles!

"Hattie, he petted that venerable yellow machine like he really loved it. 'Sweetest ride I ever had!' he said, running up the steps to go and find his parents.

"I was impressed," Paul said. "And to look so elegant after nearly sixty-five years. It's unbelievable! Seeing it sitting out there was a shot in the arm for those of us at FairAcres who've lasted through all that time, too."

I agreed.

November 11th

Today people were still talking about Al McNaughton and his car as we sat around on the porch after lunch. He had taken numerous residents—one at a time—for a spin in the little two-seater and stirred up lots of memories.

"I learned to drive on a 1915 Reo," said Grace. "I don't mean I learned to drive in 1915. I'm not *that* old! But people kept their cars longer in those days. A car was kind of a member of the family. We had a German shepherd named Fritz, and he always rode on the running board."

"Goodness!" Hazel exclaimed. "Did somebody have to reach out and hold him?"

"No," said Grace. "Never. He just hung on. Dogs were braver in those days."

"People were, too!" said Curtis. "When I think of some of the jalopies we ventured out in.... One was a Model T Ford. You could break your arm cranking it, and the radiator steamed all the time."

This reminded Paul that his family had a Model A Ford. "With a rumble seat," said Hazel. "Oh, those rumble seats!"

"Speaking of radiators," said Sidney, "I rode in a car that didn't have one!"

"What?"

"It had no radiator because it was air-cooled. Do you remember the name of it now?"

"A Franklin," somebody called out. "Ugliest car ever built. They were snub-nosed."

"I remember those mutilated-looking cars," I added. "And I remember the prettiest car ever built—in my opinion, anyway. It was the Packard." There were nods of recognition from several people as I continued. "When I was eighteen I longed for one with all my being: a silver-gray

Packard roadster with silver-colored upholstery. There was something about that long hood, with a little crease on each side, that was so genteel, so elegant."

As I continued to reminisce silently (and a little sadly) about the Packard I never owned, the talk turned to Studebakers, Maxwells, 1935 Auburn roadsters, Pierce-Arrows, Stutz-Bearcats, and even a fancy car called a Hispano-Suiza, which the Hollywood stars loved.

"I drove a Duesenberg once," said a small voice. It came from Lily Bickford, a quiet little widow from North Carolina. We all turned to her in astonishment.

"You drove a Duesenberg?"

"Yes, I did. For about an hour. I was nineteen and visiting Pinehurst. A wealthy bachelor who had a winter home there had just bought the car at the 1932 New York Automobile Show, and he was terribly proud of it. A 1932 Duesenberg! Some people say it was the finest car ever built, and they tell me that the same car I drove is still being displayed at old car shows."

"What was it like?" one of the men asked reverently.

"Oh, my goodness! I sank down in that gorgeous seat, under that big wheel, and the beautiful ornament on the hood looked like it was a half-block away! There were the fanciest buttons on the dashboard you ever saw. And I think there were seven gears."

"What was *he* like?" asked Grace.

Lily giggled. "He was sweet...but he was sixty-two years old."

"Too bad," said Grace sadly, and sighed.

Hazel spoke up. "We had the same old car for years. I think it was a Hudson. Anyway, it was big enough for all of us and two dogs. I remember when it rained we had to scramble to get those funny old isinglass curtains snapped up. We were usually soaking wet by that time."

"And remember the cars you'd pass on the side of the road, with flat tires?" Curtis asked.

"Always," said Henry. "I remember my uncle had an old, old touring car. The horn was on the outside by the driver's left hand, and when you squeezed the rubber bulb, the horn went—"

"Ah-OOOO-gah!" several people shouted, and everybody laughed. All the old horns sounded that way.

If we needed a name for the good time we had today, Dear Diary, it might be, "Where are the wheels of yesteryear?"

Before we dispersed (most of us to afternoon naps, I expect), someone took note of the date: November 11, Armistice Day.

"You don't hear much made of the occasion now," I said.

"That's true," said Paul, "but it was always commemorated when I was growing up." Heads nodded.

"The eleventh hour...of the eleventh day...of the eleventh month," remembered Sidney. "The day World War I ended."

November 13th

Some of the residents have got it in their heads that they want a "therapy pool."

"A therapy pool?" I heard someone ask. "What's the matter with our swimming pool?"

Nothing, of course. Paul used his winnings from the car-naming contest a couple of years ago to build a fine pool house and pool; but there are some residents who are afraid of the large pool.

"I'm too rickety to go in there," say several. Some very elderly are afraid of falling on the slippery border. Some said, "If we stand there in the shallow end doing our exercises, those gung-ho people doing laps will hate us."

So there has arisen a longing for a small pool holding about four feet of water in which people can safely exercise—a therapy pool. There is room for it in the pool house, fortunately.

Later

When somebody told Geneva Tinken about the idea for the therapy pool, she had a good quip: "Every time I think about exercise," she said, "I lie down until the thought goes away."

November 16th

"I'll tell you something, Hattie," said Ernestine as we finished checking our mailboxes. "Old age is just plain tacky." She was recovering from her latest dilemma: her big toenails were growing crooked and had to be removed surgically yesterday. "Crooked toenails. That's tacky."

I had to agree, and added, "Like raw places on elbows and dry, thin hair, and wobbly knees—"

"And teeth that can't handle a steak anymore—"

"And stockings that droop, and having to wear old flat, soft shoes—"

We laughed at each other and shook our heads. The list was getting too long, too sad, too tacky. After a few quiet minutes riding up the elevator, one of us said (as we always do), "But when you consider the alternative..."

There's a retired minister living here (one of several in residence) who takes umbrage when people speak that way. He says they're being disparaging. "The alternative," he is quick to remind us, "means going to our heavenly home, and what could be better than that?" Well—nothing, I guess. But not yet!

I still agree with Ernestine that much of old age is "tacky," but not all of it. There is nobility in the way some people handle the vicissitudes of late life. Nobility and inspiration. I will try to hold that thought and will try to follow the example of the noble ones.

November 20th

The problem with getting a therapy pool is, of course, how to pay for it. Several ideas have been put forth lately, and the best one seems to be an "Oddities Auction." It was Cora Hunter's idea. "We could phone all our relatives and ask them to search their attics and storerooms for old, outdated, odd, funny things," Cora suggested.

"Who will buy them?" somebody asked.

"Dealers!" Cora said. "Dealers from Charleston. Have you been to Charleston lately? It's jam-packed with tourists who are wild about antiques. People are pouring in and out of antique shops and 'specialty' shops. I've heard that the proprietors have a time keeping enough 'stuff' on hand. They'll buy almost anything, to say it came from Charleston, or at least from the Charleston area."

There were some skeptical looks, but it was decided to let Cora pursue the idea—but only *after* the holidays. She promptly formed a committee anyway, including several men. Some of the men groaned a little. Ben Chivers said, "I knew I was old...but to be on an antiques committee!"

"Oh, come on, Ben," said Cora. "We'll have fun. Wait and see. We'll dig up some things you haven't thought of in a coon's age, and they'll make you laugh, too."

"Want to bet? Like what?"

"Like cowbells or wooden legs—"

"Wooden legs?"

"Well, why not? It's an *Oddities* Auction," said Cora.

November 22nd

Paul and Curtis haven't been having their confabs out on the terrace lately. It's been too cold. But yesterday was warm and sunny. So they sat and smoked and conferred genially while I listened from the library window.

"Have you met the new lady—Virginia Lucile Somebody—from North Carolina?" Curtis asked.

"Yes," said Paul, slightly embarrassed. "She asked me to show her where the laundry room is."

"I thought she would." Curtis grinned, slapping his thigh. "That or something like, 'Would you help me get something down from my top shelf? You're soooo tall.' You have to watch out for old-time Southern double names like Virginia Lucile. They're deadly. I hear she's buried three husbands." Curtis doubled up with laughter. Paul smoked in silence.

"Do you think you'll ever marry again, Paul?" Curtis asked.

"I don't think so," was the answer. "I'll just let my record state: 'one happy marriage.'

"Sometimes, though," Paul continued, "I dream that I'm going down the aisle to meet a young woman who is waiting there, all in white, with something white on her head." He paused and chuckled. "But she always turns out to be a registered nurse, waiting to escort me into the doctor's office, or the operating room, or somewhere." We all laughed.

I saw Paul later and "caught up" on Perry Bagwell. The plan is to bring the boy here as soon as Christmas is over and let him start school in Drayton in the new year. Paul is going to contact the agency that handles foster care placements.

November 26th

The talk turned to politics today—and no wonder. All we hear about or read about right now is "The Great Election Mess" in Florida.

I think it's embarrassing. The United States: the electronic giant of the world, in a monstrous tizzy caused by a few aging voting machines and some absentee ballots. I'm sure other countries are laughing at us.

Paul had a good thought. He said, "Oh, boy! How I wish Will Rogers was still living! In a few, down-to-earth, funny words, he would gather the situation into a pungent nutshell, and so sensibly."

We all agreed. Will could have set us straight and made us laugh at the same time. There doesn't seem to be anyone today who can do that.

Emily said, "I would like to know what Harry Truman would have said about the situation."

We all nodded. Harry had good common sense.

"I wonder," Retta said musingly, "what Abraham Lincoln would have had to say about the squabble?"

All of us thought about that for a while, and then, a little dejectedly, we went to our rooms to see what CNN had to say.

November 28th

We have all gotten impatient with the political muddle, and Victor Brady decided that it was time to lift our spirits. Victor is new here. From the story he told, I think he is going to fit right in at FairAcres.

Victor said, "I'll tell you all a story about John Kennedy when he was president.

"A friend, or maybe a relative, in Ireland sent JFK a batch of beautiful woolen cloth. The president sent for his tailor, who measured the cloth and the president.

"'Well, Mr. President, I can get you a nice new suit out of this, with one pair of pants.'

"'But I've always had two pairs of trousers,' JFK said. 'Let me think about it and I'll make up my mind later.'

"The next week, Kennedy was invited to Augusta, Georgia, for three days of golf. On a whim, he took the woolen cloth with him, thinking maybe there was a smarter tailor in Augusta.

"There was. The president's hosts told him about a fine tailor named George Purdy.

"Purdy was sent for. He measured the president and

the material. 'Well, Mr. President,' the tailor said. 'I can make you a fine suit outta that nice cloth—with two pairs of pants.'

"'You can?' asked JFK delightedly. 'My tailor in Washington said he could only manage to get one pair of pants. I wonder why.'

"Purdy grinned. 'Well, I'll tell you, Mr. President. You're a lot bigger in Washin'ton than you are down heah!'"

Whoo-eeee!

December 4th

Here are some things that I'd like to have on my "Christmas list":

♣ Somebody to break in a new pair of shoes.

♣ Someone to reach for something on a top shelf.

♣ Somebody to cut my meat in tiny, tiny pieces, so that I can chew it.

♣ A memory that can hold something, and keep it straight, for longer than two minutes.

♣ Enough eyesight and flexible-enough knees and long-enough arms to enable me to cut my own toenails.

♣ Enough clout to enable me to do something about the too-loud background music that drowns out the lines on television shows.

♣ The courage to tell some loudmouth people to hush...or at least to "cool it."

December 8th

Bill Nixon was in a rare good mood at lunch today. We had been talking about some of those groups that stress genealogy—like the D.A.R., the Colonial Dames, the Sons of the American Revolution, etc.

Bill said, "You know, I should have joined the Sons of the Revolution. That would have been the nicest thing I was ever called a 'son of'."

Then, a little later, he told us about a preacher, who, when he went hunting with a group of men, would always appoint one of them to be his "designated cusser."

December 12th

The Home's newsletter came out this week and had this bit of seasonal humor in it.

Stages of Life:
1. You believe in Santa Claus.
2. You don't believe in Santa Claus.
3. You are Santa Claus.
4. You look like Santa Claus.

7

Good Spirits

December 29th

Some of us gathered together last night in F-wing parlor, where the piano is, and raised what is left of our voices in so-called "song." It would have probably sounded pathetic to outsiders, but we had a good time.

"When the Moon Comes over the Mountain" brought back memories of Kate Smith's sweet voice. Then we came up with a sad one called "Remember":

Remember, you vowed to care a lot…
But you forgot to remember.

Then somebody suggested, of all things, "I Wish I Could Shimmy Like My Sister Kate." That really took us back. When we finished singing, someone (a little younger than most of us) asked, "What's 'shimmy'?"

Oh, dear! Nobody really knew how to describe it, and certainly none of us wanted to demonstrate!

Finally, Eloise said, "I think it was kind of a dance step. You shook your body, but it had to be in time to the music."

We were satisfied, and went on with "Five Foot Two, Eyes of Blue."

We got my ragged old song book out of the piano bench and sang some Stephen Foster numbers that always make me want to cry. What a heart that man had!

We sang another tender song by another sentimental poet—Robbie Burns—about "those endearing young charms." We had just sung the line, "Thou green-crested lapwing, thy screaming forbear," when Curtis came charging in from E Hall, grinning and shouting, "Who's screaming for beer?"

That broke up the party.

December 31st

Several of us sat around the table, sipping our after-dinner coffee in quiet contentment, marking the turn of the year well before midnight.

"This is nice," said Austin Craver, lazily. "Good coffee. Good friends… The only thing that would make it better would be a little glass of Cointreau or *crème de menthe...* or some other respectable liqueur. But, I didn't see that on the menu tonight, alas."

"Alas is right," said Bill Nixon. "But I can think of a few people here—females all—who would object very vocally if such items were on the menu."

"You are right," said Austin. He grinned. "That makes me think of a woman in my hometown. Nora Newbury wasn't given, much, to any kind of jollity. For her, life was real and life was earnest, and she wasted no time trying to lighten it up, especially with anything alcoholic. Her husband, Chester, was a meek soul and went along with her.

"At a party, if someone held glasses of champagne toward the Newburys, before Chester could grab one, Nora would say very firmly, 'We don't partake.' Chester looked a trifle forlorn, as if he would like to partake; but he couldn't.

"A popular man named Ben Davidson invited Chester to his bachelors' party the night before his wedding. Nora disapproved, but for once Chester plucked up his courage and went anyway," said Austin.

"Soon after midnight, Nora heard a commotion at her front door. She opened it, and gasped. Two men were holding up Chester. He gave her the silliest of grins and a little wave with his fingers.

"Then Chester said, 'I guess there's jesh one thing to say, hon. Jesh one thing… I *partook*.'"

January 5th

At the breakfast table this morning the talk turned to breakfast cereals. I said that I'm so glad they give us hominy every morning to go with our scrambled eggs and bacon.

A lady (one of the few people here who had the misfortune to be born several states to the north) said, "Why do you call it hominy? It's grits."

"Not in my family, it isn't—or wasn't," I said, and several heads nodded.

"But, what about grits? What are they?" she asked.

"Grits is what you get when you dry the hominy and grind it," Curtis explained.

"My grandmother used to buy 'cracked' corn from the mill," someone else added. "It was ground very coarsely. Then she'd prepare it like hominy, but she called it 'hominy grits.' One of my favorite treats at her house were the patties she made out of hominy grits and fried in a big iron skillet."

"I remember my mother making hominy," said Curtis. "She soaked dry corn in lye water for several days—"

"*Lye?*" exclaimed the non-Southerner.

"Yep," nodded Curtis. "The kernels eventually swelled up and popped the skin off. Then she washed the hominy several times to remove all the lye and boiled it up. Boy, did it taste good with fresh country butter."

There were smiles around the table at the memory.

After a moment, Curtis grinned and said, "A man in my hometown shot his wife because she cooked his hominy too loose!"

Everybody whooped except the Northern lady. Curtis turned to her. "You see, ma'am, when it's too watery, or isn't cooked long enough, it's too thin. It won't stay on the fork. Some people called that 'quick-fork hominy,' because you had to eat it fast!"

Blessings on Curtis. His humor, as usual, had made my day.

January 8th

Paul called me this afternoon to say that Perry started classes today at the high school. He is in the junior class.

The boy moved into Paul's second bedroom last week. People have been very understanding, and we love to see him eating with Paul and Mr. C. in the dining room. His boyish good looks and appealing smile have already won hearts. We'll be sorry to see him go when Paul finds a place for him to live, with a nice Drayton family.

January 11th

Some people at The Home are still "with it" enough to have a computer, and to operate it. When they talk at the table about E-mail and the Internet, I just look at them in dumb confusion. And admiration.

As I've told you before, Dear Diary, I gave up on understanding electronics back when the Coca-Cola machines started giving change. You'd press the "1 Coke" button, and throw in a half-dollar, and out would come the right drink and the right change every time. (When did I last think of half-dollars, or fifty-cent pieces? Remember those? I believe one of my sons collected Kennedy half-dollars. I wonder if he still has them.) Anyway, having machines that made change was such a startling development, it troubled me a little. Things were moving too fast.

And that was the merest beginning. Now, if you don't have a fax machine and a computer, and don't speak the new technical language, you're just another Rip Van Winkle.

All of this is leading up to the fact that a woman from "way off"—who had read two of my books—sent me some pages of tidbits about old age that she had gleaned from the Internet. The items were new to me, and funny. But who wrote them? No authors were mentioned. I inquired and learned that it is "nigh onto impossible" to find the origins of the innumerable jokes that appear on the Internet.

So here goes a story (with thanks to the kind correspondent from Ohio):

Three ladies were discussing the travails of getting older. One said, "Sometimes I catch myself with a jar of mayonnaise in my hand in front of the refrigerator and can't remember whether I need to put it away or start making a sandwich."

The second lady chimed in, "Yes, sometimes I find myself on the landing of the stairs and can't remember whether I was on my way up or on my way down."

The third one responded, "Well, I'm glad I don't have your problems." She added, "Knock on wood!" and as she rapped her knuckles on the table, she told her friends, "That must be the door. I'll get it!"

January 14th

This morning in chapel we sang an old, old, old hymn: "When the Roll Is Called Up Yonder, I'll Be There." I never liked that hymn much. The writer was overconfident…doesn't say, "I'll try to be there," or "I hope to be there." He just says he'll *be* there. Good luck!

There's another old song that many people seem to love—and that I despise! Not too strong a verb. The piece is artificial and braggy. I believe the title is "In the Garden." The chorus says:

> And He walks with me
> And He talks with me
> And He tells me I am His own.

(This is the part that upsets me most.)

> And the joy we share
> As we tarry there,
> None other has ever known.

None other? No one else has ever talked to God and felt comforted? How pompous can you get?

How much better are the wise, poetic, deeply felt sentiments in such tried-and-true old hymns as:

> Abide with me
> Fast falls the eventide
> The darkness deepens
> Lord, with me abide.

Or, the magnificent:

> A mighty fortress is our God
> A bulwark never failing;
> Our helper, He, amid the flood
> Of mortal ills prevailing.

January 19th

Lying in bed last night I found myself, for no reason at all, remembering something funny I heard years and years ago.

Bert (Burt?) Parks (he who always sang, "There she is, Miss America") had his own talk show on TV for a while. One night I happened to be listening when he had a girl singer on, from the South. After she sang, he interviewed her.

"Where are you from?" he asked.

"From Round O, South Carolina."

Bert smiled. "Where is Round O, exactly?" he asked.

"Well," said the girl, "It's right close to Yemassee, and not far from Pocatalego."

That brought down the house.

Ever since then, I've been meaning to ask somebody (somebody "in the know") where the town of Round O got its name. Like a lot of my other questions it had better be asked pretty soon!

February 3rd

There are two shadows that hang over us, in retirement homes: seeing friends "go down" gradually—mentally and physically—or losing them to sudden death. I think perhaps the former is the sadder.

We experienced a sudden-death loss this week when Charles Bessinger suffered a massive stroke. A widower, Charlie had only lived here seven months, but his engaging personality, his friendliness, and love of fun had endeared him to everyone. His pleasing, true baritone voice had helped out our wavering hymn-singing on Sunday morning and at Vespers.

The chapel was jammed for his memorial service. We sang his favorite hymns (the good, strong, poetic, old ones we like), and Chaplain Brewer read a prayer by a famous early American. I'm sure Charlie loved it:

WILLIAM PENN'S PRAYER

We give back to you, O God, those whom You gave to us. You did not lose them when You gave them to us, and we do not lose them by their return to You. Your dear Son has taught us that life is eternal and love cannot die. So death is only a horizon, and a horizon is only the limit of our sight. Open our eyes to see more clearly, and draw us closer to You that we may know that we are nearer to our loved ones, who are with You. You have told us that You are preparing a place for us: Prepare us, also, for that happy place, that where You are, we may also be always, O dear Lord of life and death.

Musing.

I remember something my mother used to say when news of a death came. It was a question she had learned in the early days of her marriage when she lived in a section of lower South Carolina where the Gullah language was still heard on all sides. When someone died, her cook used to say, "Dat too bad. Did he dead hahd or easy?"

Sometimes I think of that phrase when I hear, at breakfast, that one of our residents has fled our abode, permanently, during the night. I often wonder, "Did he dead hahd or easy?" Easy, I always pray.

February 5th

Here I go again, Dear Diary, expounding against that scourge of the old century and the new: the so-called background music, which does not stay in the background. No, its chief end seems to be to obscure everything in the foreground.

I put my fingers in my ears and try to read the players' lips, but I miss "who done it" or other important last words because of that blaring noise.

I never wrote to the presidential candidates, but I wrote to my congressman. Unfortunately, he wrote me back that the government has no power to eliminate it.

I wish Harry Truman were still living, and still in the White House. He was thoughtful of old people (even his disagreeable mother-in-law). He would listen to our plea and would declare a moratorium against all obscuring, unnecessary background sounds on TV; then the happy results would soon be so evident that, henceforth, "background music" would be history.

I can dream, anyway.

February 8th

A few years ago, I developed a skin rash. Our resident physician at The Home sent me to a skin specialist in Charleston.

The specialist was a very handsome young man. Maybe that's one reason there were so many women waiting to see him.

I sat in the waiting room for an hour and a half; then I was ushered into one of his treatment rooms, where I sat for another forty minutes. At times I could hear him laughing and "goofing off" with nurses down the hall. I got madder and madder. *I'll fix him*, I decided.

Finally he came into the room, smiling and debonair. He glanced at the chart in his hand.

"Mrs.—McNair? Yes, ma'am. What is your trouble?"

I looked him straight in the eyes and said, completely seriously, "I have leprosy."

Dear Diary, I wish you could have seen his face. The debonair look was gone with the wind. I could almost hear him thinking, "I don't want to see you! I don't want to touch you!"

I let him suffer for a few seconds before I said, "April Fool!" Then I told him why I had played the trick on him.

Maybe I did some good. I understand there are not nearly as many long waits and overbookings in his office these days.

February 13th

Eloise Courtland and her cousin from Charleston have just come back from a trip to Virginia. Driving home they stopped at a restaurant near Richmond for dinner. It was a rather elegant restaurant. It even had an orchestra for dancing. While waiting for their order, Eloise decided to write a postcard to her sister. She took the card up to the desk and said to the clerk, "Do you have mail pickup here?"

"No, ma'am," he replied. "You have to bring your own date."

It happened!

8

Homes, Sweet Homes

February 15th

Good news and bad news today: The Hogans have received word that Habitat has accepted them and will probably start on their house in about two weeks. We are all thrilled, and quite a few residents have signed up to help. I'm having some difficulty imagining our "inmates" in the construction business!

The bad news is that Mike Hogan got laid off from his job. He worked for an office supply company, in the warehouse and driving their delivery truck. They let him and another worker go because orders have slowed in the "softening economy." Marybelle says he is taking it all

right because he'll now be able to spend that time working on the house. He'll look for something as soon as the
project is over.

It does seem quite unfair to me, even cruel!

Later

Cora called her committee together today to talk
about postponing the Oddities Auction until we see what
we can do to help the Hogans. I think it's a wise idea.
Sometimes our enthusiasm for helping is greater than
our energy.

February 16th

We got on an explosive subject at the table this morning: doctors' charges. There were some unbelievable tales.
Henry's was the worst.

"I went to a doctor in Charleston last year to get the
wax out of my ears. It took him about fifteen minutes.
When I went to the checkout window, the woman handed
me a bill for $125.00. I said, 'There must be some mistake.'

"She looked back at my chart and said, 'The doctor
performed a surgical procedure on you.'

"Then I remembered. While he was fiddling around
in my ear, he said, 'There's a piece of dead skin in here.'
Without changing instruments he got it out. It took
about three seconds. Some surgical procedure!

"The woman looked at my white hairs. 'Why do you
worry?' she said. 'Uncle Sam will pay for it.'

"'I hate to rip off Uncle Sam,' I told her. 'He's gonna be stripped naked pretty soon.'"

We nodded gravely.

Paul said, "There's something terribly wrong: I want doctors to make a real good living. They've worked hard to get where they are; but for them to become immensely wealthy on people's ailments…it doesn't seem right, somehow."

We all nodded.

February 17th

A resident here taught third grade in her hometown for thirty years. She told me that one day, when the pupils had received their end-of-the-year report cards and were leaving her class for the last time, one little boy stopped and looked up at her in the doorway a little sadly.

"Miz Gifford," he said to her, "you don't ever make your passin' grade, do you?"

February 21st

Perry has found ways of being useful at The Home and picking up some spending money. Arthur has put him to work part-time helping around the grounds. And he waits tables at some evening meals and on weekends.

Paul, meantime, has been trying to find a good home for the boy.

Today I had an idea.

"Paul, why don't you sound out Susie Linbaker?"

Paul's face lit up.

"Hattie, I could kiss you for that idea!"

(And to tell you the truth, Dear Diary, I wish he had!)

Susie is our head housekeeper, who lives nearby. Plump and smiling a lot, she manages to be completely efficient and popular at the same time, with both staff and residents. At about forty, her prematurely gray hair and fine complexion make her attractive.

Paul is going to talk with her and let me know what she says.

February 23rd

A happy report from Paul. Susie's response was predictably generous: "Why, sure, Mr. Chapin, we'll board that boy for a while. With three boys already, one more won't make much difference. Lordy, how those boys can eat! Especially the two that play football."

It turns out that Susie and her husband Bud, had already been thinking about becoming foster parents because their oldest son graduates from high school and goes in the Navy in June. Paul has an appointment to talk with the appropriate officials next week.

February 25th

Heard a good story after Vespers today. It seems that a number of churches in recent years have set aside a special place in their cemeteries where people's ashes can be put after cremation. (I think it's called a "columbarium," but I'm not sure of its spelling.)

Anyway, a certain elder was asked to be on the columbarium committee. He refused. When asked why, he said, "I'll tell you. I don't want my ashes thrown in that place with all the others."

"Why not?" he was asked.

"Well, you see, I'm not a good mixer."

March 1st

More to report on the Habitat undertaking: Marybelle says that Mike and Melinda are so excited and are looking forward to working on their new home. Marybelle and her husband are going to help, as are their parents. Members of the Hogans' church have made participating an official project for the congregation. Last weekend a group from the Sunday School classes cleared the lot of debris and began preparing the site for construction.

Sidney drove Retta and me by the location this afternoon. Stacks of fresh lumber and other materials have already begun to arrive.

Everybody at The Home knows about the project, and many of them have volunteered to help. Though a lot of us worked hard to clean up "Kudzu Kottage" when the Priests were moving in, I have been worried about our participation and was reassured by my conversation with Sidney. He and Retta had already discussed our "helping" with Habitat officials to make sure there would not be a problem.

"We didn't want old people falling off of ladders," said Retta.

"And we didn't want the house falling down because of people who can't see to drive the nails in correctly," agreed Sidney.

It turns out that many wonderful Habitat volunteers are "elderly," and jobs are always matched to abilities. Everyone receives training as needed, Sidney assured me. Retta explained that some volunteers, if they don't want to take part in actual construction activities, can help by providing meals to the workers. People can make sandwiches and brownies and such, and others can pack and deliver the food and beverages to the site.

March 2nd

I was telling Cora about my drive with Retta and Sidney yesterday. She is turning her Oddities Auction committee into the "Lunch Brigade" for the Habitat project.

March 5th

The first workday on the Hogans' new house was this past Saturday, and I was in the van load of people from The Home who went along to deliver lunch for the gathered crowd. We served sandwiches and drinks to the workers and watched as the foundation began to take shape.

Perry showed up, riding a bicycle Mr. C. had given him. He came over and spoke to me and others he knew and then went and pitched right in with some digging that was under way.

All was going smoothly until Geneva Tinken decided that she needed to get involved. First she insisted that she could help lay mortar on the cinderblocks. "There's nothing to it!" she said. "One of you men can just mash the block down into that squishy stuff and I'll spread some more of it on top!" She tried to commandeer a trowel from a young man, but he and others humored her out of the idea.

Then she walked over to a group of people who were moving some large pieces of lumber in preparation for beginning the framing. She got right in the middle of things, and one person almost tripped over her.

About twenty minutes later she was trying to boss around some of the church volunteers who were marking off where the front steps were to go. Mrs. Jackson, the woman who was helping to supervise the project, came quietly over to Sidney and said, "Mr. Metcalf, can you help me with Mrs. Tinken?"

The two of them conferred a moment, and Sidney promised to do something.

Canvassing the area, he spied some packages of roofing shingles. First, he walked over and got Perry and spoke to him. Then Sidney and the boy made their way over to Geneva. Sidney touched her on the shoulder, and she turned and grinned at them both.

"This is fun!" she said.

"Well, that's nice," Sidney said, taking her arm, "but there's something more important that Mrs. Jackson and I want you to do for us, Geneva. Perry's going to help you." He smiled at the young man, and a conspiratorial look passed between them. "You've met Perry, haven't you, Geneva?"

"Of course. You're that nice young fellow that I see with Paul and Mr. Cruickshank sometime."

"You two just accompany me over here, please, and let me show you what we need."

With Perry following them, Sidney led Geneva, wiping dirt off of her hands onto her pants, over to where the bundles of shingles were waiting.

"Perry is going to cut open these heavy wrappers for you, Geneva. Then we need you to count all the shingles."

"Shingles?"

"Yes. You see, the number of roofing shingles in each package is written here." Sidney pointed. "But we're never sure that there are really the correct number inside. It's important that we know exactly what we have."

She looked dubious and dissatisfied, but after Perry, who had one of those razor-blade gadgets you open boxes with, cut the paper container down the middle, she reached into the first package and started to count.

A little later, when most of us accompanied the van on its first trip back to FairAcres, Geneva was still hard at her "important" task. As we drove off, we could see her large backside, in khaki pants, reared up as she bent to her assignment.

March 12th

Today we were talking in the dining room about spring flowers, and someone mentioned sweet peas. Sweet peas always meant piano recitals to me. Whenever I played a solo in a recital—like *"Für Elise"* or "Minuet in G," or "Narcissus"—my parents would have an usher present me with sweet peas from the florist. They smelled so wonderfully sweet! Maybe having gotten safely through my "piece" made them smell sweeter to me.

"'Narcissus'…" said Annette. "I played that! It's the one where you cross your hands." She crossed her left hand over her right on the tablecloth. Several heads nodded, remembering left hand over right. We left the dining room in a glow. It's so pleasant to find that other people have the same kinds of childhood memories of things like "Narcissus" and crossed hands and sweet pea bouquets.

March 19th

Perry has moved in with the Linbaker family, and it seems to be working out fine. He has been over here frequently, getting help in his studies (algebra, especially,

I think) from Paul or Mr. C. It was a lucky day for Perry when he took refuge in Roy Cruickshank's cottage.

April 18th

The Habitat project has continued without incident and is going splendidly. Much to Sidney's relief, Geneva has not returned (though Perry has). And quite a few of our other residents have become regulars and are able to assist in a variety of ways with the actual work. Two or three are good painters—as long as they don't have to climb and balance on ladders.

Retta has lined up a group of people, including Melinda Hogan, who are going to help with the landscaping. That will be a treat for some at The Home who miss having a yard and garden in which to putter. I have joined in several times, serving the sandwiches and watching the progress of the new home.

May 2nd

The Hogans' house will be finished next weekend. Everyone has been busy, laying flooring, nailing siding, and putting up the walls. A professional plumber, as well as an electrician and a roofer are helping. Sidney said he is impressed at how much time these hardworking men give to the project, and how cheerful they are about it. The folks from The Home, he reported, even enjoy their slightly off-color humor.

*The Habitat project has continued without incident
and is going splendidly.*

At Sidney's request, I telephoned the local paper and the Charleston paper, both of whom promptly sent reporters armed with cameras. Two great articles appeared with white-haired people doing a variety of building jobs. One of the television stations then sent a crew and ran a story on the local news! Retta made everybody laugh by saying, "I do wish it had been a better hair day—for Sidney!"

The Hogans have been there constantly, and we were relieved to learn that Mike has found another job. Would you believe it, Dear Diary? He is going to work at the lumberyard that supplied the materials for the new house. What a fitting and satisfying development.

May 6th

We had a wonderful celebration this afternoon for the completion of the Hogans' house. All who had helped were there, and it was a lovely day for the dedication. Even Geneva Tinken was present, and she went around telling everyone, "I counted *all* the shingles."

Tonight some of us sat together at supper. We were full of good feelings and happy memories of the Habitat project.

"President Jimmy Carter really started something with that Habitat idea, didn't he?" somebody commented.

"Actually," said Paul, "the organization was started by Mr. Millard Fuller in Americus, Georgia. But I think Mr.

Carter has done more than anybody else to put the idea across. In my opinion," Paul continued, "Mr. Carter was a fine president, and he's the best ex-president we've ever had."

"Hear, hear!" said Sidney. "You're right about that."

There was general agreement around the table.

Then Sidney said, "I'll bet he'd be pleased if he knew that our group of old 'one-foot-in-the-grave' folks were bending our creaking bones to help build a Habitat house."

"Wouldn't he, though!" said Geneva, dreamily. "I just might write to him.... Maybe he would come over! I'd love to meet President Carter and have a chance to tell him that I helped...and that I counted *all* the shingles!"

The stars in the heavens seem to twinkle over the brick walls of FairAcres Home tonight with a special benevolence, and life has recently taken on some extra meaning. Perry has a new home and a new family, and now the Hogans have a new home. We have been involved in something of importance—and that is good.... Thank you, Lord, many of us will murmur, as we drop into a sweet sleep. It has been a good, good day.

9

Remembrance of Things Past

May 17th

Now that the home-building project is complete, Cora has turned our attention back to finding items for the Oddities Auction. It was decided to place a long table against the side wall in the dining room, bearing a sign: "Curiosities Table." This display will be just for the enjoyment of the attending folks and will contain items people don't want to sell. So far, there's a lorgnette, a buttonhook, some flypaper, and a scrimshaw pocketknife.

May 20th

Sometimes in good weather I take the "Outside Passage" in going from my apartment to the dining room. In one courtyard there is a large weeping willow tree. A few years ago when we had an ice storm I thought the old tree was done for; but it came back, rather reluctantly, it seemed to me.

I'm not sure that a weeping willow is a good tree to plant at an old-folks' home. Even in good weather it manages to look droopy and forlorn. In wet weather, like today, it is truly a sad sight.

I've about decided to stick to the "Inside Passage" and let the willow do its weeping without making my spirits droop. They're hanging a little low today.

May 22nd

Dear Diary, I was going through drawers trying to find something to contribute to the auction, and found a short story I wrote years ago. It's called "Grady Figures a Nangle." I had forgotten all about it, but I'm pleased to say the tale of two little boys still makes me laugh.

Is finding this story a sign? Last week, an old friend who used to edit our local newspaper (and who printed a few pieces of mine), sent me a nice letter and enclosed a flyer about a short-story contest. Now…what did I do with that letter?

Later

I did find the letter, but I didn't find anything "odd" enough to offer the antique dealers. I'm afraid I must have done a better job than I realized, culling things when

I moved to The Home. Perhaps Nancy or one of the boys has salvaged something from my youth. I'll inquire.

May 30th

Getting larger items for the auction has been hard, but things are coming in gradually. One bit of luck: a small museum in Marcia's hometown closed for lack of patronage, and she persuaded the directors (mostly relatives of hers) to pass on several of the items to us. They're wonderful! I shall wait to describe them to you, Dear Diary, until I make a report on the sale.

Cora has managed to get short articles about the event, which is now scheduled to be held on July 31, into three Lowcountry newspapers.

The goose hangs high!

June 1st

There was some kind of a "hitch" in the kitchen today, and we had to wait about half an hour for the dining room doors to open. It wasn't bad, though, because a number of us sat in the library and talked about the "good old days"—a subject we never seem to tire of around here. Somebody always mentions Chautauqua Week during these conversations. That took us back to the wonderful time every summer (was it one week or two?) when, in a large tent pitched in the town square, we'd be transported to a wider world by way of lectures, music, and—best of all—plays. That was something to look forward to every year.

We talked about a smaller—but dear—memory: the organ grinder with his monkey in a bright red uniform. The monkey would take off his little round cap and pass it among the crowd for the children's pennies.

"...and the knife sharpener," recalled someone, "who came around about twice a year."

"...and don't forget the ice wagon," said Paul, "with its big blocks of ice covered with something like sawdust to keep it from melting. We'd hop on the step at the back of the wagon and grab splintery pieces of ice..."

"...and tease the horses just to get the ice man's goat," put in Curtis, laughing shamelessly at his own play on words.

We do a good job of reconstructing "the good old days." They weren't all good days; but they were *our* days.

June 2nd

All morning I've been chasing a word, searching my mind for a certain synonym for "being used to." Before my eyesight got so poor I would have gone straight to my thesaurus. Through the use of a related word, I would soon have the exact word I wanted. But even if I could see, what would be a related word to "being used to"? "Accustomed to," maybe?

Later

I thought of the word at last. Many people might say, "Why spend so much time and thought over one word?" But most writers will understand and will relate to the pleasure I felt when the word finally popped into my mind: inure. To be inured to.

June 4th

A memory.

As you know, Dear Diary, I often can't remember the name of my dear friend who lives next door to me here at The Home; but I can remember every detail of things that happened eighty-plus years ago.

Such a scene came vividly to my mind today: helping with the biscuit dough. I was a tiny girl standing on a chair at our kitchen table, with a towel tied around me. Mother or the cook would take the top off of the ketchup bottle, wash it, and give it to me to cut tiny biscuits for myself. What simple fun—cutting biscuits.

June 7th

Ella McRae has told us a lot about her youngest granddaughter. Ella's daughter and her husband had thought their family was finished, and along came Lou-Anne, a ball of fire.

Ella said that last Sunday Lou-Anne, now aged four,

came to her with a pad and pencil and said, "Draw me something, Nana." Ella said she groaned. She has never been able to draw anything, not even stick-people walking down a straight road. After a minute she put down some dots and connected them with lines.

"Oh, a box!" said Lou-Anne. "Now, put somethin' in it."

Ella said she inserted the easiest thing she could think of, some round balls.

"Now, take 'em out," demanded Lou-Anne.

"The box is closed up," said Ella. "I can't get them out."

"I can," said Lou-Anne, taking the pencil and erasing the top of the box. Then she wiggled out of her grandmother's lap and darted off to another project, much to Ella's relief.

"I'm too old for grandmotherhood," she said. "Now I think great-grandmotherhood might be much better. They probably don't ask *great*-grandmothers to draw."

June 8th

My daughter called me today, all excited. "Guess what, Mom! I was going through boxes looking for auction stuff for you, and guess what I found: several of your old short stories, including a copy of 'The Gracious Thing.'"

"The what?" I asked.

"Another story you wrote years ago. About the teen canteen. Don't you remember?"

"I think I remember," I said hazily.

"I guess you gave me this copy because I figured in the story. Anyway, I read it last night and loved it. I think you should enter this one in that contest you told me about."

"Oh, dear. I had just about decided to take the plunge with the tale about Grady and his baseball."

"Well, that's a good one, too, as I remember. But please read this one before deciding, Mom. I'll bring it over tomorrow."

June 11th

I overheard Paul and Curtis talking on the terrace tonight after supper about the Oddities Auction.

"That's some nutty idea of Cora's," said Curtis.

"Yep. It's kind of crazy—but I think it might work. It's different anyway," said Paul.

"Yep, crazy," said Curtis, and they were quiet for a few moments. "You know what Cora ought to have for that sale, Paul? Some chamber pots!"

I could hear Paul slapping his knee. "You've got it, man. I can see them right now at my grandmother's house. She had no indoor plumbing, but she had the latest thing in chambers. In her guest room they were white, trimmed with red cabbage roses. There was a slop jar to match."

"And there was always a washstand," said Curtis.

"With a bowl and pitcher," said Paul, obviously enjoying his memories. "They were adorned with red roses, too."

"Sometimes there were violets," said Curtis dreamily. "The washstand had little rods for towels, and another slop jar underneath."

After a minute, Paul said, "It looks like they could have found a better name for that object.... Even as a boy I thought 'slop jar' sounded pretty terrible. But what else could they call it? Well, nowadays they would call it a disposal, I reckon.... Yep, we've got to find Cora some of those fixtures. The sale won't be complete without 'em."

They were quiet, and I knew they were smoking and enjoying the evening's peace together.

Finally Paul said, "I don't know what made me think of this story, but I always found it funny. A long time ago there was a U.S. senator from my part of the country named 'Hoar.' Senator H-O-A-R, it was spelled. Not a very pretty name, but it caused no trouble until one day when the senator read a letter from a constituent that made him hit the ceiling. The letter ended with these words: 'Give my regards to Mrs. W.'"

Whoo-eee!

June 12th

We've received several walking canes for the sale. There's one of beautiful carved wood and a carved ivory handle that will surely bring a good price. Another one has an animal's head for your hand to hold onto. It has a fierce expression with bared teeth. I don't think I would enjoy clutching it.

My own walking cane is no *objet d'art*. It is made of perfectly plain metal (aluminum, I think) and has no real beauty. But it's sturdy, and its curved head fits my hand just right. As one of my children said when small, "I'm used of it."

Like David's "rod and staff," it comforts me.

June 14th

Musing.

There are many small indignities about old age that are "off-putting" and truly annoying.

I believe my arms have shrunk even more this year. My sleeves hang down more than halfway over my hands. Awkward and revolting and tacky.

If I could see, I would thread a needle and take tucks in the sleeves. As it is, I just have to let them hang.

Then there are shoes. I was always a little vain about my shoes. My feet are slender (quadruple A), and I used to buy fine, slim shoes with a little heel and sometimes a small leather bow.

Now I wear clodhoppers—huge, flat, shapeless things that hug the ground and are practically fall-proof.

On the rare occasions when I dress up, these days, I smile a lot and hope that people's eyes won't wander down to those ugly moccasins, where my feet meet the floor.... Vanity, thy name is Old Woman.

June 15th

The two worst things about my loss of eyesight are: not being able to see the faces of my two precious great-grandchildren, and not being able to read books.

I've been an avid reader since the first grade. People used to say I would wear my eyes "plumb out," and maybe I did (although my doctors say "no"). I made tracks to our Carnegie Library nearly every day. What a joy to open a new book by an author you had made friends with before!

A few years ago I had to graduate (or descend?) to large-print books, which are great. But sometimes even those letters don't seem tall enough for me, so I now rely on Books on Tape. These are marvelous unless the reader's voice turns into a squeal or a growl in the middle of a line, which often happens. Or unless the voice says, "Turn the cassette over," which you do, and nothing happens at all. Blankness. Frustrating.

I get tapes sent to me by the State Library—a wonderful service when the tapes work.

The other day I put in a tape by a Southern author, and I soon realized that a mistake had been made in choosing a Yankee lady to read the piece. She was plainly unfamiliar with our sounds and sayings. She couldn't say "kudzu." She had probably never heard of that vicious vine that can shroud even the tallest pine trees in our Southern landscape. She called it "kood-zoo." However, she did have very clear diction and pronounced every syllable of every word, and I was grateful to her for that.

June 18th

Sometimes, Dear Diary, when my children have hovered over me more than usual, and been free with their advice and suggestions, I find myself wanting to say, "Oh, leave me alone." But then I think, "You'd better not. They might do it."

June 20th

After hearing me describe the fancy walking canes we have collected, one of my sons has given me a replacement for the aluminum Wal-Mart one I've been using. I didn't have the heart to tell him I liked my plain one just fine. The new one is carved (no animal teeth, thank goodness), handsome, and heavy. Woe betide any pickpocket who bothers this old lady!

I suppose I will soon "graduate" to a walker. I don't look forward to that. They are too large and clumsy. And what do you do with them when you sit down?

The next step after a walker is a wheelchair. A lady resident at The Home recently acquired a "jazzy" one—of the motorized variety. She gets in the hall and opens it up! We scatter out of the way, like chickens in the road!

June 21st

I had a very nice visit this first-day-of-summer afternoon with Dr. Templeton and his sweet wife, Francine. Dr. Templeton is a retired Presbyterian minister, much beloved by the people of the churches he has served. I always enjoy their company, but I'll never forget an event that happened not too long after they arrived here.

We were tablemates, and one night at supper the good doctor said, "I rented a movie today that sounds like a winner: *Through the Fields of Clover.* Doesn't that sound nice? Frannie and I would like it if you all would come over and watch it with us."

He was so eager we couldn't turn him down.

"Curtain rises at eight," he said, obviously pleased.

Four of us strolled over to the Templetons' cottage later, anticipating a wholesome evening. Our host and hostess had placed chairs just right for viewing. Most of us don't have a lot of company these days, and this was to be a treat, for them and for us.

What it turned out to be was a disaster. The film was not only suggestive and pornographic; it was downright evil.

Francine has very poor hearing, so her husband rents films that are captioned. Therefore, we not only had to see and hear the filth, we had to read the words, plainly printed below. (This was back when my sight and hearing were much better.)

We began to squirm and look at each other. Finally Dr. Templeton looked at us and said, "Do you friends mind if I turn off the machine?"

We breathed a sigh of relief. I'm sure our faces were red, with our host and hostess having the reddest of all.

Francine served coffee and cake, and we talked about everything we could think of...except dirty movies. I expect the good doctor had a private preview before inviting guests again.

10

An Old Story

June 22nd

I now have to wear hearing aids in both ears. When I go to the "clinic" here (the nurses' station) to get the batteries changed—which I can't see to do—I think of my Aunt Flora. She was very deaf, and used an "Acoustican," an early hearing aid. It was a small box that sat in her lap and had wires going to her ears.

One day I was talking into her Acoustican, and she suddenly turned the switch off.

"Don't cut me off right in the middle of a sentence, Aunt Flo," I yelled. My feelings were hurt.

"Child," she replied, "the batteries for this thing cost

me fifty cents a day—and many days I don't hear fifty cents' worth!"

I was put in my place.

June 23rd

Last night I had a treat: a rerun of *Fiddler on the Roof* on TV. At one point, Tevye (was that his name?) was begging God to straighten out something that was going wrong in his life. Suddenly he said, looking heavenward, "God, I wonder, who do you take your troubles to?"

It gave me pause.

Later

Thinking of Tevye's (and God's) troubles brought up a memory.

My mother was born in a small Alabama town, just a few years after the Civil War ended. She told me tales of the time. Some were tales of hardships, but more were stories about funny people. I believe there were more "characters" then than there are now.

Mama said she was walking "up town" one day, skipping along; but she slowed down as she approached the Willoughby house. Boney Willoughby was on the front porch, and the children found Boney interesting. He had been injured in "the Waw," and was "not right in the head."

Mama said she "squinched down" behind the fence's palings and listened. Boney paced back and forth, shaking his head, moaning and saying, "Pa gone. Mule dead." Just those four words, over and over.

"Pa gone. Mule dead."

He made them sound like the tag end of misery.

Mama said she told her family about it at supper, and it became a family saying. Our family loves "sayings," especially funny ones. After that, whenever a situation was dire or sad, somebody would shake his head and say, gloomily, "Pa gone. Mule dead," meaning, "It's the pits. Nothing can be worse than this."

Poor Boney. Nobody could replace his Pa. I hope he found another mule somewhere.

June 25th

There has been much speculation about our sale next month. Some of the residents, mostly men, think that we are silly to try to make money out of "crazy old junk."

One of them was overheard to say, "They ought to auction off Geneva Tinken. She's an oddity, if there ever was one."

Later

I have been "on the fence" about whether or not to enter that story competition. After lunch I got up my nerve and asked our esteemed administrator, Mr. Detwiler, if he would read "Grady Figures a Nangle" and "The Gracious Thing," which Nancy brought over, and help me decide which one (if either!) to enter in the short-story contest. Entries must be postmarked by Saturday.

June 26th

Mr. D. brought the manuscripts back to me today.

"I stayed up late last night, and I really thoroughly enjoyed both of 'em. Most fun I've had in a long time."

Bless him.

"Do you think one is good enough to send to the contest?" I asked. "I feel a little silly entering with people half my age…probably even younger than that."

He smiled. "They could wish they had half your talent."

"You think so?"

"I do, indeed. 'The Gracious Thing' took me back. Reminded me of my father. It's great, but if I were you, I'd send in the 'Grady' story. I really felt for those two rascally boys trying to recover their lost ball. It's hilarious and touching, too. Please send it in."

I told him I probably would. I value his advice.

June 27th

We were reminiscing today, while some of us were organizing auction items, and I was thinking back to the days when I could see. "I loved my old Underwood type-writer," I commented.

"Now, that would make a good auction item, if you had just kept it," said Cora.

"It was big and noisy, but it never gave me the trouble that computers seem to give." I said. "I just fed it new ribbons every now and then, and it clanked away faithfully. I declare, I don't believe you can even buy carbon paper any more! That seems terrible to me. I don't like it. Things are changing too fast. There used to be a sameness, an order, about things."

"I didn't have any trouble reading your old typed stories, Hattie," said Cora. "You're a good typist."

"I should be. I spent six months at business school after college. I loved typing...and Mr. Gregg's shorthand."

"I did, too," said Ernestine. "I still use shorthand when I want to take down part of a speech on TV or something. Those little squiggles are so satisfactory."

"I liked them, too," I said. "I wonder if they even teach shorthand any more."

"I know what you mean," said Ben Chivers, who, after complaining about being on the committee, had pitched in and been a big help. "I'll bet soon you won't be able to get shoestrings. They'll tell you that all the shoes have to be zipped up."

"Or stuck together with Velcro, or something," said Cora.

We were showing our age today.

June 28th

Several friends who have read my stories agree with Mr. Detwiler about sending in the Grady one. I perused it again slowly and laughed. It *is* funny, if dated. (Of course, why wouldn't it be? I wrote it decades ago!) Should I enter? Or shouldn't I? I hope I'm not just being foolish.

June 30th

I put "Grady Figures a Nangle" in the mail today. We shall see, Dear Diary. It's kind of fun to be in competition again.

July 1st

The subject of the short talk at Vespers tonight was "Prayer." Walking home to my apartment afterwards I thought about the first prayer I had ever learned, the ubiquitous, beloved, "Now I lay me down to sleep...."

Naturally, I taught my children to say these same words each night; but when Nancy was about six years old, she told me one bedtime that two lines in the prayer bothered her. Scared her. They were the lines, "If I should die before I wake, I pray thee Lord, my soul to take."

I spoke to her brothers about the prayer, and they said they didn't like those two lines, either. So I announced to them that hereafter they could omit all reference to dying in the night. Instead, they could substitute these words: "When in the morning light I wake, Help me the path of love to take."

I was not the author of the words. I found them in a letter to the editor from another mother, printed in some church magazine or other. Anyway, my children liked the suggestion.

I'm too crippled up to kneel these nights; but as I crawl under the covers I often begin my supplications with the cherished, "Now I lay me down to sleep" prayer. I use the original version. In my case, it's comforting and proper.

July 4th

I lay in bed this morning wondering if there would be any special goings-on today to take note of our country's birthday. I chuckled when I remembered how several of our ladies had tried to commemorate the Fourth a few years ago—before we got our swimming pool.

Laurie Maxton, fairly new at the time, had persuaded some residents to join a water aerobics class with her at a nearby spa. The last class session was to be July 3, and Laurie wanted to celebrate. The day before the class, she spied a brightly painted stand on the side of the road, with cars packed around it: "Fireworks!" said a myriad of signs.

Sparklers! thought Laurie. And she pulled in and bought some.

When the group gathered at the side of the pool the next day, Laurie, full of patriotic fervor, insisted that everyone stand at the edge of the water with sparklers and sing "God Bless America."

She lit the little metallic sticks and commanded, "Now sing!" The gray-haired ladies loved their country, so they did their wavering best.

Before they could finish the first verse, pandemonium broke out. Fumes from the gunpowder (or whatever made the sparkles) got into the air system and floated through the building, setting off the smoke alarms. The manager came tearing into the poolroom and was horrified to see that each sparkler was dropping a black residue into the water.

Class was cancelled and the pool closed, to be drained and cleaned.

"Believe me, I'll never try to do any star-spangling again," Laurie told me.

And I don't think she has.

Later

Once again I'm lucky about my tablemates this go-round. I'm sitting with Paul, Sidney and Retta, and two more nice people. Today the conversation revolved around our great country and all things patriotic. Though both Sidney and Paul were in the Army Air Force in World War II, they don't talk much about their personal experiences.

Tonight, however, Paul offered an interesting theory about what he called "the two worst wars in history."

He was turning his water glass around and around, and then he said, "I feel that WWI and WWII were caused by one man's slight physical imperfection."

We were all ears.

"What man?" asked Retta.

"Kaiser Wilhelm. Wilhelm von Hohenzollern. He was born with what we used to call a 'withered arm.' I don't think it was really withered—just a few inches shorter than his other arm. At any rate, it is said that he felt the handicap terribly. He apparently was convinced that to make up for his deformity, he had to overachieve.

"I believe that it was this very strong feeling in him," said Paul, "that caused his aggressiveness...that caused him to raise a mighty army and challenge the world. And in that mighty army was a super-Germanic corporal named Adolf Hitler, who worshipped his Kaiser and never got over that gentleman's defeat.

"Hitler brooded about his fatherland, and he resented the peace treaty. He thought the reparations were unfair and brutal, and he became obsessed with all this, trying to find a way to put *Deutschland über Alles*—Germany above all others. He brooded...and he acted, with a result too awful to describe."

We sat thinking about Paul's conjecture. It made sense. If the Kaiser's arm (right? left?) had been normal, he would no doubt have been a more normal person—less hungry for power. And his follower Adolph Hitler might have been less brooding, less obsessed.

It's something to think about.

July 7th

Some time ago one of my sons saw me squinting at my large wristwatch, and still not being able to see the numbers. He ordered me a wristwatch from Japan. It's also large, but it has another feature: A nice Japanese lady lives in it and tells me the time whenever I press a certain spot. She has a little trouble saying "eleven." It sounds more like "weven"; but I know what she means. Now, if she would only tell me the day and date.

The first time I wore the new watch, a rooster started to crow at ten minutes after five. Scared me to death! *"Cock-a-doodle-doo-oo-oo!"* the rooster crowed loudly! I finally realized it was the alarm, and that somehow the alarm had been set by accident. I didn't know how to un-set it, so I got used to hearing the cheerful little fellow telling me it was cocktail time.

One day I went to a special service in the chapel at five o'clock, forgetting about my "alarmist." Our nice chaplain was in the midst of a prayer when, right on time, my little friend began to crow. Loud. I put my right hand over my left sleeve, but he crowed on, cheerily.

All bowed heads were turned toward me. I didn't know how to cut him off.

If I had been able to see clearly enough to get the watch off of my wrist quickly, I would have sat on it. I put my arm under my jacket. He crowed right on. *Cock-a-doodle-doo-oo.* I was getting up to leave when he finally stopped crowing. The minister finished his prayer and looked in my direction wonderingly.

I got someone to un-set the alarm, but it makes me a bit sad. I probably will never hear my little rooster friend again telling me happily that it is cocktail time. Oh, me!

July 19th

I wonder if anybody in the world remembers the words to a song I learned about seventy years ago. I recall the lines:

> Oh, there's nothing half so sweet in life,
> as love's young dream....

I can pick out the tune on the piano, but the rest of the words elude me and it's driving me crazy.

Later

Why would I want to remember a song that recalls one of the saddest times in my life? The breakup of my first love affair.

Don't talk to me about the joys of youth. There were those, but there were also wounds that stabbed so deep they left scars.

I will stop thinking about that song. I will go to the

Country Store, get a Coca-Cola, and ask somebody to tell me a good joke. Life's too short for grieving.

Later still

I heard not one, but several good jokes this afternoon:
♣ Families are like fudge…mostly sweet, with a few nuts.
♣ Today's mighty oak is just yesterday's nut that held its ground.
♣ Freedom of the press means no-iron clothes.
♣ Inside some of us is a thin person struggling to get out, but she can usually be sedated with a few pieces of chocolate cake.

July 20th

If you have to be ninety percent blind and half crippled, this is a good place to "be it in." A lot of dear people here seem to have my welfare on their minds. My hope is that, like Shakespeare's quality of mercy, their goodness will be "twice blessed"; that they will receive a rewarding feeling of benevolence for having helped a Poor Old Soul to tie her shoe or button her blouse or take the right turn in the hallway.

There is always a lot to be thankful for, if you take the time to look. For example, I'm sitting here thinking how nice it is that wrinkles don't hurt.

11

Odds and Ends

August 1st

I'm happy to tell you, Dear Diary, that the Oddities Auction was a great success. It was fun, too. Mr. Detwiler had studied the items to be auctioned, and he had lots of witty things to say about them.

The place was jammed. More than a hundred extra chairs had been brought in. They were filled, and many people were leaning against the wall. Quite a number of the attendees were dealers from Charleston and several other Lowcountry towns.

There was a great deal of interest in the "Curiosities Table." People were "taken back" by the sight of such things as a corset, a "sadiron," and the knife with a handle of carved scrimshaw. There was also a cloche hat of soft, blue felt and a lady's fox fur neckpiece, the kind with the fox's mouth clamped to its tail.

As the crowd was gathering, Lewis Trenholm, a resident, picked up the corset and asked, "What is this?"

"It's a corset," his wife told him, looking somewhat embarrassed.

Suddenly, Paul called out from the other end of the table, "I'll give you a hundred dollars, Mr. Detwiler, if Lewis Trenholm will model that corset."

Mr. Trenholm, who is a tall, thin man, fortunately had a sense of humor. His wife helped him put on the garment, and he carried it off well. In the best Paris fashion modeling manner, he made his way around the room, the supporters dangling and jingling as he strutted. This started the auction off in a spirit of fun.

Mr. Detwiler banged his gavel and greeted the crowd cordially. He told everyone how anxious we were to get a therapy pool in which to take exercises—and which could be used as a whirlpool.

Before the first sale item was brought out, Mr. D. motioned to four residents sitting together on the front row. They arose, turned to the audience, and burst into song.

Mr. Trenholm made his way around the room, the supporters dangling and jingling as he strutted.

Daisy, Daisy, give me your answer true.
I'm half crazy, all for the love of you!
It won't be a stylish marriage.
I can't afford a carriage.
But you'll look sweet upon the seat
Of a bicycle built for two.

As they sang the last line, Arthur rolled out a tandem bike from the door of the storage room. It was painted bright orange, and the two leather-covered seats were highly polished. As he rolled it around the platform, the crowd applauded.

Mr. Detwiler asked for bids, and they came with alacrity. I squeezed Cora's hand. We were doing all right.

People gave each other puzzled looks when Arthur produced the next item. It was a heavy, round piece of copper and brass with a long wooden handle.

"Want to guess?" asked Mr. D., holding the object up. Nobody answered, so he opened up the round end.

"It's a bedwarmer!" someone shouted.

"Right you are, sir!" said Mr. Detwiler, holding it open. "Here is what held the hot coals."

He closed it and pushed it back and forth, as if warming a sheet.

"This thing guarantees you'll have the warmest bed in South Carolina, and if you've got somebody to keep you warm—and don't need this heater—see how fine it will look on your wall!"

He closed the warmer and held it up against the wall. It looked quite handsome, and apparently the audience thought so, too, because the bidding was brisk.

Arthur next brought out something in a fancy box. Mr. Detwiler lifted it out.

"Remember these, folks? I'll bet your grandmother had one on the center table in her parlor."

Several heads nodded at the sight of a stereopticon.

"And here, in the smaller box," continued Mr. D., "are the slides." He lowered his voice to a confidential tone and picked out one slide from the box. "I'll tell you something, folks. If any of you spent your honeymoon at Niagara Falls, now you can gaze at the slide and see what the Falls look like."

There were guffaws from the men and tittering among the ladies. One of our ladies blushed. "Why, Mr. Detwiler!" she said.

After the stereopticon came, among other things, a walking cane with a bicycle bell on it, a "hall tree" for hanging hats, and a quaint baby carriage that had no top, just a tiny umbrella covered in eyelet embroidery and ruffles. After it sold, Mr. D. declared an intermission (he wanted his mid-afternoon Coca-Cola, I'm sure) and asked the people to have fun perusing the Curiosities Table. I heard them exclaiming over the items displayed there.

The first item brought in after intermission was an ancient tricycle. It had a huge front wheel and tiny back wheels. There was a hard wooden seat, with no leather and no springs.

"Look at this, ladies and gentlemen," said Mr. D. "In England these were called 'penny farthings.' Don't ask me why.... Who'll give me some money for it?"

Apparently the dealers considered it a good find. They vied with each other, bidding, and it brought a nice sum.

After several more items—including two chamber pots courtesy of Paul and Curtis—Mr. Detwiler rapped his gavel for quiet.

"Now, here's something very special, people!" Mr. D. held up a pair of men's knickerbockers. They were of plaid wool and obviously buckled below the knee. "This is a pair of Bobby Jones's own golf knickers, worn by him on the No. 2 course at Pinehurst in 1938. These are authentic, folks. Bill Nixon, one of our residents, has a brother who owns a golf course and golf museum. He very kindly donated these pants. They are made of the finest Scottish wool."

He ran his fingers over the material.

"Some man here ought to have these. Maybe they would improve his game."

There were bids from several of the men, but one of the Charleston dealers won out.

Those dealers were really sitting up and taking notice

now, and a ripple of excitement went through the audience when the next thing to be auctioned was produced. Many had heard of this item.

It was a framed piece of newsprint, with a headline in letters three inches high, proclaiming:

THE UNION
IS
DISSOLVED

Mr. D. held the relic up for all to see. "Folks, this is a famous headline and the actual front page from *The Charleston Mercury* for December 20, 1860. It announces that South Carolina had seceded from the United States, and the text describes the action taken that day by the Secession Convention meeting in the South Carolina Hall in Charleston.

"Only a few copies of this issue survive, and they are considered extremely valuable by historians and collectors. It has been well preserved with museum-quality framing. Otherwise the newsprint would probably have deteriorated."

"How did you get it?" called out somebody in the audience.

"One of our dear residents, who asked to remain anonymous, had it hanging on the wall of his room," was the answer. "He told me that if he had any grandchildren, we wouldn't be getting it. This is a piece of history, ladies and gentlemen. What am I bid for it?"

Hands went up. Voices called out. The dealers were in a frenzy. I heard one of them say, "I've been hunting for one of those for years!"

That bidder was finally able to get it, but for a goodly sum.

"I paid too much," he said, grinning from ear to ear, "but I've got a customer who'll pay me more."

The last few items brought out were kind of an anti-climax. There was a man's walnut lap desk, a turn-of-the-century telephone, and an autographed first edition of Helen Hunt Jackson's *Ramona*.

Mr. D. thanked everyone for coming and for parting with their cash.

"One of our gentlemen has written down your purchases," he said. "You can settle with him at the table over there."

After the visitors had left, carrying their "loot," the auction committee held a meeting. We had a good time counting the money, which turned out to be much more than we had hoped for.

"I told you!" said Bill Nixon gleefully. "An auction is the best kind of sale. You want something a little bit, and then somebody else wants it, and suddenly you want it a lot! Of course, just seeing Lewis model that corset with the dangling supporters made the day worthwhile for me."

We thanked our beloved administrator for the great job he had done as auctioneer.

"Think nothing of it," he said. "I had a good time—and for a good cause. And I tell you something: I think maybe now I can persuade the company" (we knew he meant the people in Charlotte who own The Home) "to put out enough money to finish the job. So—I'm pretty sure you can count on exercising safely and having whirlpool baths in a few months."

We wanted to hug him. Some of us did.

August 10th

Recently, the Chaplain's Office sponsored a "Planning Session," which I attended. As Chaplain Brewer asked us to do, I wrote down a few words of instruction about my "last rites." I wrote that I wanted a simple graveside service, with only one addition: I want Dr. Stamforth, a retired minister with a great voice, to read the words of the following poem.

BE STILL, MY SOUL

Be still, my soul: the Lord is on thy side;
Bear patiently the cross of grief or pain;

Leave to thy God to order and provide;
In every change He faithful will remain.
Be still, my soul: thy best, thy heavenly Friend
Through thorny ways leads to a joyful end.

Be still, my soul: thy God doth undertake
To guide the future as He has the past.
Thy hope, thy confidence let nothing shake;
All now mysterious shall be bright at last.
Be still, my soul: the waves and winds still know
His voice who ruled them while He dwelt below.

Be still, my soul, the hour is hastening on
When we will be forever with the Lord,
When disappointment, grief, and fear are gone,
Sorrow forgot, love's purest joys restored.
Be still, my soul: when change and tears are past,
All safe and blessed we shall meet at last.

These wonderful words were adapted from Psalm 46 by Katharina von Schlegel. We often sing them in church to the tune "Finlandia" by Jean Sibelius.

August 17th

Earlier this evening there was a terrific electrical storm, and the sky turned dark as midnight. The power went off, to my great annoyance. Tom Brokaw was right in the middle of telling me something of importance in his clear, attractive voice.

My flashlight was in the bedroom, and I was afraid to stumble in there to get it; so I sat huddled in my recliner feeling sorry for myself, and a little scared.

This was a "hissy" of a storm, as people used to say. There were bolts of lightning that seemed to part the earth, followed by thunder with all the stops out—a scary, unbelievable cacophony. The fury seemed aimed at me. "What have I done, God?" I murmured.

Sitting there, huddled and lonely, I suddenly began to wish for Ophelia. I could see her clearly in my mind, through the steam that the iron sent up. She stood behind the ironing board, a solid, safe figure to me, a child of six or seven years sitting and watching her. Ophelia had been working for us as long as I could remember. When we weren't talking, she sang. One of her favorites was:

> I couldn't hear nobody pray, Lord.
> I couldn't hear nobody pray.
> Way down yonder by myself
> And I couldn't hear nobody pray.

The song was plaintive and sad, but I liked it. Mama always said that I was born with a "good ear," and even at that young age I had some appreciation of the sweet, true, tender quality of Ophelia's voice. It did something to my heart.

When there was a thunderstorm, Ophelia would come around to my chair and take me into her lap. I loved it. She had a vast, soft bosom that was comforting to lean against, and she smelled good, like bread dough and freshly ironed clothes.

"Old Marster goin' about His bizness," she'd say. "We got to be quiet." But she wouldn't be completely quiet. She'd sing softly, and I'd snuggle up, and the terrible noises outside weren't scary any more.

On this stormy night, I longed for her strong arms, and even the sad song, "I couldn't hear nobody pray...." She died years ago, and I hope she is hearing all the prayers she wants to hear in her heavenly home free from troubles.

The storm finally petered out. "Old Marster" finished his business. The lights came on, and the TV blared (I had forgotten to turn it off). Tom Brokaw had finished, but there was *Jeopardy* to look forward to.

I wiped the nostalgia out of my eyes, and settled down to be confounded by the amazing knowledge of Alex Trebek's contestants. Maybe this would be one of the grand, rare nights when I knew the answer to Final Jeopardy and they didn't!

August 18th

Paul and Curtis were outrageous tonight, in their after-supper chat on the terrace.

When I saw them headed that way, I hurried to the library and hid behind a curtain at the window to listen, as usual.

The two men talked about last night's sharp thunderstorm and the humidity that had been heavy all day. "Well, that covers the weather," said Paul. "Now I suppose we should talk about crops."

"Only crop I know of around here," said Curtis, "is Bill Stroman's tomatoes. He's got two pots of 'em on his patio outside his apartment. Bearin', too. Loaded."

"He'll be able to sell 'em," said Paul. "Nothing like a vine-ripened tomato."

The two men were quiet for a little while. I was about to leave my perch, disappointed, when I heard Curtis start chuckling.

"What's up?" asked Paul.

Curtis proceeded to tell something that I should not repeat, even to you, Dear Diary; but it's too good to withhold. Forgive me, Mama…wherever you are.

"I just happened to recollect a crazy story," said Curtis. "It's about a country couple who went to town to see a doctor, because the wife had been droopy lately. The doc gave her a thorough examination, and then he called the husband in.

"'Well, sir,' the doctor said, 'she *is* "droopy." Her body and spirits are at a low ebb. She needs a great deal of stimulation, including regular sexual intercourse.'

"'Really?' the husband asked, blinking hard at the doctor.

"'Yes. I would recommend three times a week. Say...Monday, Wednesday, and Friday.'

"The husband scratched his chin. 'Well, I'll tell you, Doc...I can bring her in on Mondays and Wednesdays, but on Fridays she'll have to take the bus.'"

Paul whooped, and I had to put a hand over my mouth. That Curtis! If he isn't something.

August 31st

Today there was an official looking envelope from SEAA (the Southeastern Authors Association) in my mailbox. Inside the envelope was a certificate stating that I had won first prize in their short-story writing contest and a letter from the judges congratulating me and telling me that they had had to choose from among more than four hundred entries!

I stopped by Mr. Detwiler's office on the way to lunch to pass along the news and to thank him for his assistance and encouragement. He asked my permission to announce the award at lunchtime. A number of people stopped by the table to congratulate me, and several asked to read the story. It will eventually appear in the association's annual anthology, but Mr. D. suggested we put it in the next FairAcres newsletter. I'll take him a copy tomorrow, Dear Diary. And now, Goodnight.

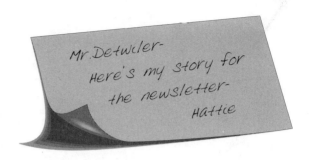

"Grady Figures a Nangle"
A Short Story by Hattie Patterson McNair

The boy lay on his stomach, his chin on his arms, surveying his bailiwick again, more in the role of a bored watchman than of an explorer. He was all too familiar with every molehill in this yard, every broken piece of fence, every dog-dug hole that made the grass harder to mow.

There was never anything different. He used to think that an Indian might be lurking behind the big live-oak tree, waiting with "bow'narrow" for an enemy to show his pale face; but Grady knew now that that was kid stuff.

His eyes squinted at a whitewashed building beyond the Japanese plum tree. *I wish I had as much money as I know how far it is to the woodpile.*

He worried an ant with a piece of pinestraw for a while. His bird dog, Marshal Dillon, lying beside Grady, rolled on his back to scratch himself in the grass. Grady searched him idly for fleas and ticks, but soon decided even this was too much of an effort in the ninety-degree heat. He picked up his baseball glove and banged his fist into the deep pocket, then rolled over on his back and looked up at the summer clouds.

Miss V'ginia said not to have mean thoughts, but how kin you he'p it? 'Specially with people like Miz Quillen around.... I wish I knew whether Pop was stingy or whether he jes' can't remember bein' nearly ten an' needin' a baseball.... I couldn't he'p losin' those others. If Mr. Mac would cut his old kudzu vines off the back lot, I'll bet I could find a zillion balls.... When I grow up and have little boys I'm gonna give 'em a new ball ev'ry day an' two on Sundays. An' they won't hafta mow any old grass or take out any old gobbidge to get 'em either.

He slammed fist into glove again, looking sadly into the pocket that seemed to him to beg out loud for a white spheroid to fill it.

He heard a familiar "Bob-Bob-White" whistle and was answering it when his best friend Tank appeared around the corner of the house. The boy's nickname, derived from Tankersly Dubose Guerrard the Third, was appropriate to his size. Grady's father had once said, "Tank was designed when meat was cheap."

"Boy!" Tank said, falling down beside Grady and rubbing his fat stomach. "Did we have a dinner *t'day!* Baked chicken an' 'sparagus an' corn fritters *an'* peach cobbler! An' all *fresh.*"

"Whaddya mean, all fresh?" asked Grady. "You 'customed to eatin' gobbidge?"

"Aw, I mean nothin' frozen or made out o' ready-mix. You wanta hear why?"

"I reck'n so. You're gonna tell me anyway."

"Well, m'Daddy blew his stack yest'day at th' table. Boy, did he blow! First off, at dinner Mama had frozen fish—you know those little sticks—an' m'Daddy said they tasted like sponge. An' then at supper he pushed aroun' th' stuff on his plate that came outa one o' those mix-up dishes in the oven—whaddya call 'em?"

"Cashroles, or sump'm."

"Yeah. Well, he picked out frozen spinach an' sardines an' noodles—"

"Erp!" said Grady, gagging.

"—an' then he th'ew his fork down. *Blam!* Mama cried an' said th' picture looked real purty in th' magazine, an' m'Daddy said, Yeah, that was th' trouble—too dern many magazine resipees an' ten-minute dinners bein' tried out on him. He said he was sick o' tearoom tripe, and he wanted some honest-to-John rations for a change. He said he didn't want to find a Lord's thawed thing on his plate, ever again. An' he said he wanted a chicken for dinner t'day that was walkin' aroun' this mornin'."

"Whew! He evermo' laid it on, didn't he?" said Grady admiringly.

"Yeah—and it worked! We et high off th' hog t'day. *Man!*" Tank rubbed his stomach some more, and licked his lips.

"Didja hit your Pop up for a new ball while he was full?" asked Grady.

"Well...no. Y'see, Mama, she was still sore. She banged pots aroun' all mornin', with her lips stickin' out 'bout a mile; an' so m'Daddy, even tho' he et like he was perishin', he still knows things're kinda ticklish, an' he lef' for th' plant 'fore I could ketch him."

"You're so snake-diggin' slow. Didja ask your Mom?"

"*Foot.* She wouldn't-a give me a *spit*-ball t'day... I reck'n we might's well give up."

"Not me. I'm gonna get me th' money for a new Big Nine Official some way, or else I'm gonna get my ole one out uv Old Lady Quillen's yard. I'll figure a nangle."

"Yeah. You kin do it. 'Member that time you figured a nangle 'bout gettin' us invited to th' Baptist picnic?" Both boys chuckled at the memory of Grady's cleverness. "An' 'member when you thought up 'bout chargin' people to go up in our tree house?... Sa-a-ay, you reck'n we could work that one again?"

"Naw. Mama'd raise Cain. Jes' because Rudy fell out an' broke his ole arm."

The boys lay quietly for a while. Finally Tank turned toward his friend and said in a low voice, "How much we got in the treas'ry now, Grade?"

"I forget. Le's go see."

They went in the back door of the house and down a hall.

"Sh-h! Don't wake up ole Tike from his nap. He'd pester us t'death."

They tiptoed past the younger brother's room and into Grady's room, where he took down from a shelf a shoe box marked:

CLub BiZnESS

The contents of the box, when emptied on the bed, consisted of a pile of nickels, five turkey feathers on head bands, a few odd marbles, some "tattoos" left from an Easter-egg-dying kit, two melted chocolate drops in the bottom of a bag, and a notebook.

The boys counted the nickels. "...seb'mty-five, eighty, eighty-five, *ninety!*" said Tank, and ran his plump hands greedily through the pile. "Ninety cents. Not enuff for a Big Nine, but it'd buy a Junior Boy's.... You reck'n we could kinda borrow it, Grade? You're treas'rer."

"How'd we pay it back?"

"I don't know." Tank's round face looked solemn. "My Aunt Eva gives me a dollar ev'ry birthday...but that's not 'til November."

Grady turned to the first page in the notebook.

CLuB RuLes

You can't be abcent without you are sick.

You must be Loyel and True.

You must stick by your fethered Brothers.

Bring 5¢ ($.05) cents dews to every meeting.

The tresuror has to keep the dews until
   the Club desides to have a party.

Chee, what kid stuff, thought Grady, who had written the rules. *I was eight, and couldn't even spell feathered.* Aloud he said, turning to the only "fethered Brother" present, "How long since we had a party, Tank?"

"Lemme see. 'Bout Easter, wasn't it?"

"Yeah... An' they're liable to start talkin' party agin before we kin pay back... Besides, I oughtn't to."

"Oughtn't to what?"

"Break Rule Five. I couldn't look Miss V'ginia in th' face."

"Who's she?"

"Miss V'ginia? You don't know her? Man, you oughta be a Prezbaterian. She's the purtiest Sunday School teacher in town. She's so purty an' so nice, she's got me readin' th' Bible—th' begats an' all."

"Chee!" Tank was impressed.

Grady looked at his pal studiously. "I'll bet you don't even know th' Golden Rule."

"Th' Golden Rule?" Tank scratched his head. "Lemme see... 'God Bless Our Home'?"

Grady rolled his eyes and sighed.

"You 'Piscopalians!" he said scornfully, putting the "dews" back in the box and the box on the shelf. "Come on. Call Marshall. Le's go up town."

Going "up town," a distance of about seven blocks from Grady Furman's house, would mean a brisk ten-minute walk for some people; but a brisk walk is not for almost-ten-year-old boys. Various things must be checked on—behind trees, up trees, in ditches, in abandoned pieces of sewer pipe. Tank and Grady made all the usual investigations, with the dog for advance detective.

In the hot quiet of early afternoon, they seemed to have the town to themselves. They picked a quince from a limb hanging over Judge Mortimer's fence, and used it for a ball, pitching and catching a winding way up the street.

They hid behind a bush in front of Rudy Grainger's house and sang out: "Cutie, cutie, Aw, Rudy!" in the highest, most feminine voices they could muster. At last their "feathered Brother" came down the steps dejectedly. He had begged his mother not to call him "Cutie" in front of his pals.

"Aw, cut that out," said Rudy. "'S no use to ask me t'go anywhere. I can't."

"Why not?"

"Mama's payin' me a quarter to mind Stinker."

"Huh!" said Grady. "You're broke out with luck. I hafta sit with ole Tike for *nothin'*."

"Where're you fellas goin'?"

"To the gettin' place, I reck'n," answered Tank. "Only we don't know where it is. We're tryin' to figure a nangle on gettin' us a baseball."

"You hab'm seen any balls comin' back over th' fence?" Grady asked, indicating with his head the Quillen yard next door.

"Huh! You think *she'd* th'ow anybody's ball back to anybody? Not 'nless she could hit somebody side th' head with it, an' knock 'em windin'."

Grady shook his head in wonder, as he and Tank went out of the gate. *How could anybody be*

*that dog mean? Not to let you in the yard to even
look for your ball?*

The boys lingered in front of Mrs. Quillen's
fence. They got behind a tree on her sidewalk and
pretended to shoot out every windowpane in her
house, furnishing their own sound effects. *Ping.
Crash. Ping. Crash. Ping. Crash.* Then Tank
switched to a heavier gun. *Bang-yow!*

"I think I got 'er that time," he said. "We'd better beat it b'fore th' sheriff gets here."

They raced away, but slowed down in the next
block. It was too hot for even fugitives to run. They
sat on the curb, their spirits drooping.

"I wish m'Uncle Frank was here," said Tank.

"Why?"

"*He'd* give us a ball. He's always givin' boys
things 'cause he don't have one. A boy, I mean.
An' maybe it's a good thing he don't have one,
'cause he's not married. But he lives way over in
Looziana.... He bought him two parrots for company, an' guess what he named 'em? He 'mem-
bered sump'm he read in th' Saddy Evenin' Post
a long time ago, an' he named 'em 'Hork an'
Spit'!"

"*What?*"

"You know. Like this." Tank cleared his throat
and spat. "Hork an' Spit!"

Grady howled with laughter. "I sure would like
to meet your Uncle Frank!"

They found sticks and played them against the
iron rails of the Methodist Church fence. They

peeped through at the tombstones, studying them apprehensively.

"Grade, why d'ya reck'n so many of those folks were scared to death?"

"What?"

"Well, you look. It says sump'm 'bout 'scared' on nearly ev'ry stone."

Grady began to laugh. In spite of the awesome nearness of the cemetery, he laughed until he rolled on the sidewalk.

Tank's eyes got big. He looked from his convulsed friend back to the tombstones, fearful that such disrespect would bring on some kind of ghostly censure.

Finally Grady sat up and wiped his eyes.

"Tank'sly Guerrard, I'll swanny! You are th' *dumbest.* It's *'Sa-cred'...*'Sacred to th' Mem'ry Of.' Don't you know anything?... Come on, dumbie. Le's go see Mr. Willie." He whistled for Marshal Dillon, who was nosing around in the churchyard. "Maybe he kin give us a s'gestion 'bout how t' get a ball. Maybe he'll pay us sump'm to sweep out th' store."

"Yeah, le's do. He might give us some Tootsie Rolls, anyway."

"All you ever think about is your snake-diggin' stomach."

"Tha's not so. I he'p Mr. Willie plenty uv times for *nothin'.* I *like* him. Mama likes to trade with him 'cause he calls her 'Girl' an' 'Young Lady.' M'Daddy says she'd walk a mile further an' pay a dollar more, anytime, to hear that."

They reached the town square and turned in under a sign that said: "Wm. Palmer, Gro." and found their friend half asleep in his folding chair in front of the bread rack.

"Well, if it's not Hambone!" said Mr. Willie. "And Hot Shot." He had his own nicknames for all the small fry, among whom he was a favorite. Like Grady's beloved Miss Virginia, he had a satisfying way of listening to them and treating them with a respect to which they were not accustomed. "Next to customers with money, I'd ruther see you gentlemen than anybody I know. He'p yo'selves to some candy."

Before the last syllable was out of his mouth, Tank had the glass door of the candy counter open and was blissfully selecting an assortment.

Grady hunched himself up on a counter and sat there frowning.

"Whatza matter, boy? What you so drop-lipped about?" asked the grocer.

"Mr. Willie, what would you do if you knocked a baseball—your last baseball—over a fence into a ole lady's yard an' she wouldn't even letcha come in th' yard to *look* for it?"

Mr. Willie slapped his thigh. "I'd go to the sheriff an' get me a search warrant," he said.

"Not if it wuz Miz Quillen, you wouldn't, I betcha."

"You're right, boy. Not if it wuz Madge Quillen." He shook his gray-thatched head. "Th' idea. Keepin' a boy's ball... I tell you what I'd do, if I wuz you fellas. I'd *worry* that old nanny goat into givin' my ball back."

"But how?"

"Well, I'd hang aroun' her place like Grant hung aroun' Richmon'. Let's see… She raises cats, don't she?" Grady nodded. "Well…maybe you could ketch holt uv one uv her cats, some kinda how, an' hold it for hostage. How 'bout that?"

Grady's eyes lit up. "Come on, Tank! We got work to do! Thank you a *heap,* Mr. Willie…Hey! I gotta idea! Cats like fish. If we had sump'm fishy—"

"I got jest th' thing," said the grocer, getting up and taking a can from a shelf. He opened it and with his pocketknife lifted five or six sardines into a paper bag. "I'll contribute these to the campaign. Good luck, men."

Grady, Tank, and Marshal Dillon reached the door at the same instant, and boys fell over dog.

"Drat that stupid ole dog!" said Tank, picking himself up.

"Don't you cuss my dog!" warned Grady.

"Well, I don't see how we're gonna ketch a cat-hostich with *him* along."

The boys looked questioningly at Mr. Willie, who smiled and shrugged.

"Okay, I'll keep 'im. I'll get a bone out of th' cold room and give it to him in th' back alley. Here, Marshal!"

The boys thanked him and raced out. In five minutes they were in front of Madge Quillen's house again, peeping through the picket fence at her old-fashioned hodgepodge of a yard. Flower beds were bordered with bottles. Bushes had been planted any and everywhere, with no thought of a plan. There was even an old pit, where potted plants had once spent the winters. There were hundreds of places where a baseball could be hiding.

Suddenly amid the bushes a black-clad figure took shape and advanced on the boys from behind a phalanx of cats.

Madge Quillen frowned and shook her trowel at them. "What d'you want *now?*" she asked.

"We—we were jes' tryin' to see if we could see our ball, Miz Quillen."

"*Your* ball?" She looked from one boy to the other, glaringly. "*Whose* ball?"

"His an' mine. We went halfs on it... Won't you *please*-ma'am let us come in an' look for it?" pleaded Grady.

"It'd would be a waste of time to look for it, for I've already found it."

"You *have?* Could we please-ma'am have it back then?"

"You may not. I'm tired of things being hurled into my premises. I'll have to teach you a lesson. Now run along."

"But if we promused not to play ball at Rudy's anymore—just at my house—I live *way* off—"

"No. And that's *all. No.* Now run along. Make haste. *Run.*"

They ran, but not far. From behind an oleander bush down the street they watched their adversary go into the house, without her cats, and shut the front door.

"She leaves 'em out sometimes for air, or sump'm," whispered Tank. "I'll bet they need it, an' th' house too." He held his nose.

After a few minutes, the boys crept back, crouching low. Thick foliage shielded them from the house. Grady took a sardine out of his pocket and held it between two palings.

"Kitty, Kitty. Here Kitty!"

To his delight a showy white cat, about half grown, rose to the bait. Grady jerked the sardine back just in time. The cat squeezed her head through the fence. Grady gave her another sniff of the fish, then stuck his hand between the palings and eased her through. Still crouching, with his prize held tight against his chest, he hurried around the corner and leaned against a tree.

Tank came panting up. He patted the cat. "Man, we got us a good'un! I've heard her call this white one 'Presh.' Whatta we do now? Send a ransom note?"

"Not chet. Gotta let 'er get missed first."

"Where kin we hide out?"

"I'm thinkin'... Hey, I know! At Miss V'ginia's! Come on."

When the boys came near Virginia Godwin's house, they saw her getting out of a car at the curb. Grady glared at the young man behind the wheel as he drove off, feeling the first pangs of jealousy.

His teacher saw him and her face lit up.

"Hi, Grady!"

"Hi, Miss V'ginia!"

"Who's your friend?"

"This is Tank, Tank'sly Guerrard."

"Hi, Tank, and who's *this?*" she asked, taking the cat from Grady's arms.

"This is Precious. She's our hostich!" answered Tank eagerly.

"Your *what?* Come on in and tell me about it."

"Who was *that?*" asked Grady, pointing toward the car that had just driven off.

"Oh, that was Joe Kinsley, a friend of mine. "Why?"

Grady shrugged unhappily and made no reply. *I wish she'd wait for me to grow up.*

On the Godwin's screened porch they shut all doors and put the cat down to roam. Grady told Virginia about the angle they were trying to work.

"But, Grady, that's kidnapping!"

"Cat-nappin,' y'mean!" quipped Tank, which struck the three of them as extremely funny.

When he could stop laughing, Grady said, "Well, it's what she gets for ball-nappin'."

Virginia dried her eyes and tried to put on a serious expression. "Wait a minute, Grady. There's a difference. Your ball landed in Mrs. Quillen's yard. She didn't do anything to get it there. But you lured her cat out, now didn't you?"

"Well—"

"Suppose somebody did that to your dog and took him off?"

The boy's eyes opened wide at this new thought. "But Mr. Willie said—"

"I know. Mr. Willie was trying to help you all out. But we've got to think about poor old Mrs. Quillen too."

"Poor old Miz *Buzzard,*" spat out Tank.

"I know she's cranky," agreed Virginia, "but she hasn't had much of a life. Her husband died, you know, just a few months after they were married. If he'd lived, and they'd had children, I'll bet she would be a different somebody.... Do you know why she wears those funny old dresses? Because she doesn't have the money to buy any new ones. She stays on in that dark house by herself, just kind of nursing her grief—"

"An' nursin' 'bout a zillion cats. How kin anybody like cats better than kids?" asked Tank.

"Well, one thing's for sure," announced Grady. "She'll have a zillion-minus-one tonight."

"Grady!" Virginia leveled her soft hazel eyes on him. "She calls the roll at bedtime, I've heard. She probably couldn't sleep...."

"Let 'er miss it a while. We've missed our ball long enough. When she hands over our ball, we'll hand over her ole Precious."

"Yeah!" agreed Tank. "An eye for an eye, an' a tooth for a tooth!" He puffed up mightily. "I'll betcha didn't know *that* one, Prezba*teer*ian!" he flung at Grady.

Virginia fixed some refreshments to soften the boys up for a little persuading she felt she must do. While she served them, they told her the Hork an' Spit story, which brought on another round of merriment. When they were happily having second helpings of lemonade and cookies, she eased up to the matter at hand.

"Have you boys ever heard the saying, 'You can catch more flies with honey than with vinegar'?"

"What does *zat* mean?" asked Tank.

"It means that if you try being really extra polite and nice to people like Mrs. Quillen—"

"We did!" said Grady. "I said, 'please ma'am' to her two times."

"The trouble is, not many boys in town have been nice to her. They've been mean—throwing rocks on her porch, taking off her gate, banging up her garbage can. Bully-type boys. If she wasn't small and old and alone, they wouldn't dare.... If we could just show her that there are some other kinds of boys besides bullies... Grady, you remember last month we studied the Golden Rule. Now if some people were holding your dog, what would you have them do?"

He raised up belligerently. "They'd better not do anything unto *him*—'cept let him go! Do you think we oughta jes' let this cat go?"

"No. I think you should knock on Mrs. Quillen's door and say that her cat got out and you've brought it back. If you do it nicely, she might—she just *might*—return your ball. Will you please try?"

"S'pose she feels like she's gotta get all th' facks?" asked Tank shrewdly. "Like how ole Precious got th'ew th' ole fence by herself?"

"Maybe she'll be so glad to have her kitty home—"

"I'll do it," broke in Grady, who had been thinking hard, "if I kin have two condishuns. I want a big paper bag to put this wiggletail of a cat in, an' I wanta write out a note to th'ow at that ole gal if she runs us off th' place. I got sump'm to say to her."

Virginia had misgivings, but she brought him a bag, and paper and pencil. He insisted on writing the note privately and without censorship. He folded it, put it in his pocket, and put the cat in the bag.

"Thanks a lot for th' lemonade an' stuff, Miss V'ginia," Grady said as the boys went down the steps. "See you in church!"

"You'd better! And please let me know what happens, Grady!"

They nodded and waved. Virginia watched the two lovable, barefoot figures and their bag full of squirmy "hostich" until they turned the corner.

A frown crossed her luminous face. She suddenly felt terribly young and inexperienced. She had had no training for Sunday School work, no course in child psychology. All she had was love, and sympathy. *Dear Lord, please open up Mrs. Quillen's heart. Please let them get their ball back. The way people treat them means so much more than anything I can teach them....*

She went back inside, and her eye fell on the pencil Grady had written with. *Now what in the world did he say in that note? I'm that curious!*

Her newest young friend was discussing her at this moment.

"Gol-*lee!*" said Tank, trotting along. "She's th' *greatest.* Where'd ja ever find a Sunday School teacher like *that?* Y'oughta see mine. She's 'bout ninety-five, an' her teeth are yellow as punkins. One minute she's all ooey-gooey: 'How are my sweet little dahlin's this mawnin'?' an' th' nex' minute she's snarlin' atcha for some li'l ole thing like havin' a flyin' squirrel in your pocket at church... But Miss V'*ginia!* Boy! Who-*whooooo!*" His wolf whistle was immature, but emphatic.

Grady said nothing. For some reason, he didn't particularly relish having his idol praised by his fat little friend. She was *his* teacher... *I wish I had told her about not takin' th' club dues,* he thought, *when I so easily could of.*

When they reached Mrs. Quillen's yard, they removed a wire hoop that fit over the gatepost. They raised a latch and lifted a hook which finally allowed the creaky gate to open about halfway. They slipped in and closed the gate carefully.

"Now you let *me* do th' talkin'," ordered Grady as they went up the walk.

"You're welcome to, man. In fac', I'd jes' ez soon go home right now—" Tank turned around, but Grady, nearly dropping the bag, caught him and pushed him up the steps.

They could see cats in every windowsill, looking out; and in one window they saw the mistress of the cats, gazing at them malevolently.

"Yikes!" breathed Tank at the sight of the wrinkled face, and he would have run away but for the strong clutch on his arm.

The door opened before they could knock.

"Gracious peace! Get off my place! I *told* you—"

At this moment Mrs. Quillen heard a distinct "mee-ow" coming from the paper bag Grady was holding, and her hand went to her breast.

"Miz Quillen, one of your cats got out, an' we've got her here for you—"

"Precious!" shouted Madge Quillen as he lifted her white pet out of the bag. "Oh, Presh! Pretty Presh! You've been gone for two whole hours. I thought sure you were dead—"

She held the cat to her flat bosom tenderly. As she stroked the white fur, her chin trembled and a tear landed on the wrinkle under each eye.

The sight of the twitching chin and those wet wrinkles did something to Grady. *All this over a lost cat! She sure must be hard up for sump'm to love.* Words that Miss Virginia had used came back to him: *lonely...poor...nursing her grief.* He took a deep breath.

"Miz Quillen, y'know what Tank an' me could

do? We could take some chicken wire an' string it inside yo' fence, so even the little kittens couldn't get th'ew!"

Two pairs of eyes looked at him in astonishment: Tank's round, guileless ones, and the woman's old, distrustful ones.

"Now, listen here—" Madge Quillen frowned. She was sure this was some kind of trick.

Grady took another deep breath. He felt big and broken out with kindness all of a sudden. It was a good feeling.

"An' you know what else? We could rake your yard out for you sometimes!"

Mrs. Quillen looked at him closely. "I don't have any money to pay you," she said.

"Oh, that's okay. We don't have much t'do in th' summertime. We'd do it for nothin', wouldn't we, Tank?"

Tank's tongue was apparently paralyzed. He stood gaping until Grady pinched him in the seat.

"Yikes! Yeah! Sure."

Mrs. Quillen had not taken her eyes from Grady's face. "Boy, are you making these offers to me just to get your ball back?"

Tank nodded vigorously.

"No, *ma'am*," said Grady. "I'll *swanny*, ma'am. We'll be *glad* to he'p you. You kin keep th' ole ball."

And he meant it.

Suddenly, for a reason he couldn't explain, nothing mattered as much as having this poor soul look at him with liking.

Which is exactly what began to happen. As Tank described it to his mother that night, "It was like th' wolf turnin' into th' Grandma, instead of th' other way aroun'! Boy, did she soften up! An' th' sweeter she got, th' sweeter Grady got. Whew! I thought I'd hafta go suck a lemon. Anyway, we got our ball back. But you know what, Mama? He says we've *still* gotta go work in her ole yard. For *nothin'*. Anyway, *he's* gonna work for nothin'. I held out 'til he promused me a rabbit's foot an' a arrowhead, to he'p him."

Tank didn't relate to his mother the ending of the afternoon's episode. After they had latched, bolted, and hooked the gate and started home, Grady took the folded note out of his pocket and read it.

"Lemme see it, Grade! Lemme see whatcha wrote," begged Tank.

Instead, Grady shook his head and began to tear the note up. This was too much for Tank. He snatched the pieces out of his friend's hand and ran. He managed to make it to his own yard and to take a quick look at a few of the pieces before Grady wrestled him to the ground and got them away.

Afterward, he could only remember seeing "Ole cheet," and "Ole Meany Quillen." What else the note had said he would never know. He would not even ask; for he understood that his friend was existing at present on some sort of higher and nobler plane, a plane which Tank neither expected nor wanted to reach for a while yet. He liked things pretty well where he was, especially now that the food and the domestic relations at his house had improved simultaneously.

"And," Tank said to himself, "we got our ball back.... Sometimes that Grady Furman makes me mad 'nuff to hork an' spit—but I hafta admit he sure worked things right t'day. And *I'm* gonna get a rabbit's foot an' a arrowhead jes' for doin' a good deed. Sometimes I kin figure *me* a nangle too!"

The End